WOOF!

Allan Ahlberg

WOOF!

Pictures by Fritz Wegner

Published by
The Trumpet Club

666 Fifth Avenue
New York, New York 10103

Text copyright © 1986 by Allan Ahlberg
Illustrations copyright © 1986 by Fritz Wegner

Dell ® TM 681510, Dell Publishing, a division of the Bantam Doubleday Dell Publishing Group, Inc.
RL: 5.0

ISBN: 0-440-84007-4

Reprinted by arrangement with Viking Penguin Inc.

Printed in the United States of America

April 1988

10 9 8 7 6 5 4 3 2

KRI

For
my mum
and Oldbury

Contents

1

This Happened

There was once a boy who turned into a dog. This doesn't happen every day. If it did, the world would soon be short of boys and overrun with dogs. What's more, it would hardly be a story worth telling. It would be like: There was once a boy who had his breakfast; or: There was once a boy who walked down the road. Luckily – for story-tellers, at least – that isn't the way of it. There are common happenings in this world, and uncommon. So . . .

There was once a boy who turned into a dog. The boy's name was Eric Banks; he was ten years old. The dog he turned into was a Norfolk terrier.

Eric Banks was a quiet boy, most of the time: 'steady worker', 'methodical', his school reports said. He was the kind of boy who didn't make a rush for the back seat of the bus, or go mad when the first snow fell. He was left-handed, right-footed and rather small for his age. He had freckles.

Eric lived with his parents and his little sister; her name was Emily, she was three. His dad was a postman; his mum had a part-time job in a shop. Eric himself had a paper-round which he shared with his friend, Roy Ackerman. (Actually, he was too young to have the round. It belonged to his cousin. But she had broken her arm, and Eric's dad was a friend of the newsagent ... so, Eric was standing in.)

Eric first turned into a dog a little at a time in his own bed. His parents were downstairs watching television. His sister was fast asleep in the next room. The time was ten past nine; the day, Wednesday; the month, June. Until then it had been a normal day for Eric. He'd done his paper-round with Roy, and gone to school. He'd had two helpings of his favourite dinner. He'd played with Emily before tea, and Roy after. He'd watched television, had a shower and gone to bed. Now he was *in* bed and turning into a dog.

It happened like this. Eric was lying on his side with his eyes closed. He was almost asleep. Suddenly, he felt an itch inside the collar of his pyjama jacket. This – although he didn't know it yet – was the fur sprouting. He felt a curious tingling in his hands and feet. This was his hands and feet turning into paws. He felt his nose becoming cold and wet, his ears becoming flappy. Eric opened his eyes. He didn't panic straight away. This was his nature, partly, but also he was still half-asleep. The thought in his mind was: 'I'm turning into a dog!'

That was another thing about Eric: he was a good guesser. When Emily first learned to talk, it was usually Eric who guessed what she was trying to say. He could guess the mood his teacher was in, just from the way she held her hymn-book in assembly. Now – on the evidence of a furry paw where his hand should have been – he guessed he was turning into a dog. He didn't suppose he was turning into a *were-wolf*, for instance, which is what Roy Ackerman would have thought. He didn't suppose he was dreaming, either, which he was not.

The time it took Eric to turn into a dog – his shape blurring and rippling like a swimmer under water – was about fifteen seconds. The time it took him to become frantic was about five seconds after that. His first action was to begin scrabbling in the bed, trying to get a better look at himself. His thoughts were in a turmoil: 'I'm a dog! A *dog*!' The next thing he did was try to get out of bed. This wasn't easy for a dog in pyjamas; besides, they were baggy on him now. Eric leapt, and landed in a heap. He kicked his way clear of the trousers and backed out of the jacket. He resisted the urge to growl when one of his claws got caught in a buttonhole. He sat on the floor and thought: 'I'm a dog!'

It was now a quarter past nine. The last of the evening sunlight was shining through the green curtains. Everything in the room – furniture and wallpaper, Eric's books and toys, his junior science kit, his clothes laid out on a chair beside the bed –

was tinged with green light. Birds were chirruping outside the window. Next door, Mr Phipps was mowing his lawn.

Eric got to his feet – all four of them – and walked uncertainly across the room. He put his front paws on the dressing-table and stared into the mirror. A furry, rather surprised-looking face stared back. 'I

don't believe it,' he thought, and then: 'I look like a Norfolk terrier.' Eric knew a bit about dogs. He'd done a project on them with Roy in the second year.

Once more Eric sat on the floor. He was bewildered, to say the least. A confusion of questions jostled in his head: 'How could it happen? What's the cause of it? Why me?' He went to the window, put his paws on the sill, ducked his head under the curtain and looked out. Mr Phipps was emptying the grass cuttings onto a compost heap. A whisp of blue smoke was rising from a bonfire in the next garden along. Eric left the window, and – with no clear aim in mind – nudged open the bedroom door with his head. He went onto the landing. He couldn't see much – it was gloomy – but he could smell all kinds of things. There were biscuit crumbs in the carpet. There was talcum powder. He felt the urge to sniff around. Soon he came upon a chocolate button which his sister must have dropped. She had been eating them earlier that evening. Eric studied the button. At that moment the thought in his mind was: 'Being a dog might not be *all* bad.' And he ate it up.

2

Shoo!

Eric sat at the top of the stairs. He had sniffed around for other chocolate buttons without success. He'd been tempted to try his luck in Emily's room — her door was ajar as usual — but decided not to risk it. Besides, the prospects weren't good. Emily dropping her sweets was common; Emily leaving them was rare.

Now Eric cocked his head on one side. From the room below he could hear the television. In the kitchen his dad was making supper. There was a smell of coffee and cold meat. Eric felt his mouth watering, and — all at once — came to a decision: he would tell his mum and dad, that was the thing to do! After all, it wasn't as if he'd done anything wrong; wrong had been done to him.

Eric began to go downstairs. The thought occurred to him: 'I wonder what's on?' And then: 'Perhaps I can stay up, since I'm a dog.' But going down stairs isn't easy for a dog, especially an inexperienced one. Eric found his stomach was dragging on the steps and being tickled by the carpet. What was worse, his back legs kept catching up with his front. On the last few steps he took a tumble, skidded on the hall mat and bumped into the coat-stand. After that, the sitting-room door opened, the hall light

14

went on – it was gloomy there, too – and Eric's mum appeared.

Mrs Banks looked down at him. 'Charles!' she called. 'We've got a dog in the house!'

A moment later Mr Banks appeared in the kitchen doorway. He saw a worried-looking Norfolk terrier on the hall mat. (Mr Banks knew about dogs. He was a postman, remember.) He crouched down and held out a hand. 'Now then,' he said; 'how did *you* get in?'

Eric peered up at his parents. He was surprised to see how enormous they were. Their feet were huge; their heads up near the ceiling. And he was surprised that they didn't know him. Of course, there was a good reason for this, but even so . . .

Eric advanced towards his father's outstretched hand and began to speak. 'I didn't get in, Dad – it's me, Eric – I've turned into a dog!'

Well, that's certainly what Eric meant to say. It's what was in his mind. However, what came out was just a string of barks and yelps. Eric tried again. It was no use. The trouble was, he had the brains of a boy, the thoughts of a boy, but the vocal chords of a dog. Mr Banks patted his head. It occurred to him that he had seen this dog before. Its expression was . . . familiar.

Now Eric, in desperation, began prancing about. He had the idea of somehow *miming* who he was, or at least showing his parents that here was no ordinary dog. The effect was convincingly dog-like. Mrs Banks patted him also. 'It's almost like he was trying to tell us something,' she said. (She was a good guesser, too; unfortunately, on this occasion, not good enough.)

'Yes,' said Mr Banks. 'Perhaps he's trying to tell us how he got in.' He took hold of Eric by the scruff of the neck and began leading him towards the door. 'Come on, out you go!'

Eric didn't like the sound of this. He barked and whined. He dragged his feet.

'Sh!' said Mrs Banks. 'Bad dog – you'll wake the children!'

'I *am* the children,' barked Eric, 'or one of them – or I was!' He struggled on a little longer. Then, sensing the hopelessness of the situation (he could hardly bite his own father), Eric gave up. He allowed himself to be led from the house and down the front path. Mrs Banks went on ahead and opened the gate. Mr Banks pushed him out onto the pavement.

'Off you go,' he said, and clapped his hands. 'Shoo!'

Reluctantly, Eric shuffled off a few steps, then sat down. When his parents' backs were turned, he pushed his head through a gap in the fence. He watched them as they returned to the house. He heard his mum say, 'I wonder how he *did* get in?' He saw the front door close.

Eric rested his muzzle on the bottom rail of the fence, and felt hard done by. A warm breeze ruffled the fur along his back. Garden smells assailed his nose. He pricked his ears to catch the distant chiming of an ice-cream van. Someone across the road was playing a piano; someone was laughing. Eric stared forlornly at his own front door. He began to think of ways to get back in.

Just then a young cat came sauntering round the corner out of Clay Street. The cat saw Eric and Eric saw the cat more or less at the same time. The cat, though inexperienced, knew what was called for: it turned and ran. Eric didn't hesitate either. Here he was, a dog; abandoned on the street by his own parents *because* he was a dog. What else was he to do? It wasn't his fault. He ran after the cat.

Eric didn't catch the cat, though he tried hard enough. He chased it down Clay Street and into Apollo Road. He almost cornered it by the Ebenezer Chapel. He only lost it at the scout hut. At the scout hut, the cat left the pavement and ran up an eight-foot fence instead. (An older cat would have done something of the kind sooner.) Eric skidded to a halt. He barked and pranced about at the foot of the fence. The cat glared at him from the top, swished its tail and disappeared.

Eric stopped prancing. He barked half-heartedly at the spot where the cat had been. Now that he had time to think, he was embarrassed. He looked up and down the street to see if anyone was watching. He had his tongue out, panting – more embarrassment! Across the street, a man and a dog came out of one of the houses. Eric recognized the dog. It was a bull-mastiff he sometimes had trouble with on his paper-round. His dad had trouble with it, too. The mastiff spotted him and began barking fiercely and

straining on its lead. Eric couldn't understand the barks in detail, but the general meaning was clear. When he could see which way the man and dog were going, he hurried off in the opposite direction. From a safe distance he allowed himself a defiant bark for the mastiff's benefit.

Eric trotted on. He glanced back once or twice to check that he was not pursued. He began to think about his troubles. 'That cat distracted me. I've got no reason to be running the streets.' He was in Vernon Street now, and heading up towards the park. 'Yet if I go home, I'll get put out again.'

Eric slowed down and finally stopped. He looked around in a baffled way. There was an interesting smell of sausage roll in the air. He ignored it. Overhead the sky was cloudless and full of light, though it was getting late, half-past nine at least. Suddenly, Eric thought of something. He remembered the writing he'd seen scrawled on the fence which the cat had run up: DOWN WITH THE VILLA, P.L. LOVES R.V., and so on. He remembered reading it. Well – and this was the point – if he could read, he could *write*. He could go home and scratch a message in the dirt: 'S.O.S. ERIC' or just 'ERIC', that would do. 'Mum and Dad aren't stupid,' he thought. 'They'd never get rid of a dog who could write their own son's name in the –' he had another idea '– Emily's sandpit, that was the place!'

Eric at once became impatient to try out his idea. Luckily, on Vernon Street there were grass verges between the front gardens and the pavement. He soon found a bare patch suitable for his purpose. He looked around. Two girls with tennis rackets were coming down the street. He waited for them to pass. A woman with a pram went by on the opposite side. A car and a couple of cyclists came and went. Then it was clear.

Eric sat up straight and extended his left paw. He brushed a sweet-paper and a bit of twig from his chosen spot. He began to write. 'E...R...,' he scratched his letters in the dusty earth. It reminded him of the sand-tray at Mrs Parry's playschool years

ago. 'It's going to work,' he thought. 'E . . . R . . . I . . . C
. . . I can do it!'

When he'd finished, Eric put his head on one side
and stared at the result. 'Needs to be neater, though
– that R's no good.' He scrubbed out what he had
written and began again. He became for a time
engrossed in the quality of his writing. (If Mrs
Jessop – she was his teacher – could've seen him
then! Eric was not always so particular.)

All of a sudden he was aware of being watched. He
heard a voice say, 'Here, Jack – come and look at
this dog!' From the nearby garden a large woman
was peering at him over a hedge. She had her hair in
rollers and was holding a watering can. 'He's writing – in the dirt!'

From the direction of the house a man's voice said,
'Geroff!'

'Yes he is – he's stopped now – he's scrubbing it
out!'

'Geroff!' said the man.

Eric considered the situation, and decided to
leave. He set off up the street. 'E . . . R . . . I . . . C,' he
heard the woman say. '"Eric", that's what he wrote.'

'Geroff!' the man said. There was a burst of
laughter. 'That's no name for a dog!'

3

Purnell's Fish Shop

Eric arrived at the park gates in good spirits. If that woman could read his writing, so could his mum and dad. He was in a hurry to get home and decided to take a short cut through the park.

Eric trotted through the gates and past the park-keeper's house. He saw a notice saying: ALL DOGS MUST BE ON A LEAD. He quickened his pace. As he followed the path towards the pond, he was aware of smelling things *before* he saw them. The flower-beds, for instance; the new paint on the bandstand; a litter-bin, even. Eric resisted the urge to snuffle *in* the litter-bin, and kept going. Soon he caught the aroma of tobacco smoke and fish bait, and came to the pond.

The last fishermen were packing up their rods and other gear. One of them was smoking a pipe. One was tipping a tin of worms onto an earth bank. Eric came up behind him. He'd dug worms from that bank himself, many times. He watched the worms go wriggling away. He felt the urge to kick his back legs in the dirt, and did so.

Now Eric followed the curve of the pond. He overtook a man and a woman walking arm in arm. A big boy on a bike overtook him. The smell of water – he *could* smell it – made him realize how thirsty he was. It was all that panting. But Eric had no wish to drink at the pond, though dogs did drink at it. There were crisp bags and Coca-Cola cans floating there. Usually, when he and Roy played football, they drank at the fountain. It was an old-fashioned one, with a metal cup on a chain and – if he remembered rightly – a dog trough.

Eric left the pond and made a detour to the fountain. He had to cross the cricket pitches and climb a hill. By this time there was hardly anyone about. He approached the fountain, lowered his head and – a little self-consciously – began to lap the water. It tasted good; it tasted different. Eric thought about this. The chocolate button had tasted different too, he recalled, though it was hard to say what the difference was. He paused and rested a while: lapping was hard work. A man in a track-suit went running by and made him jump. Eric drank a little more. He shook the drops of water from his furry chin. He sat back on his haunches.

The park was now deserted. Overhead, the sky was turning an ever darker shade of blue, with red and brown and duck-egg green where the sun had set. A few stars were shining. Eric stared up at the sky. 'I'm a dog,' he thought. 'Why *is* that? What's going on?' He tried to remember the dog project he'd done in the second year. Perhaps there was a clue there. He thought of stories he'd had in the infants, where a witch would turn a prince she didn't like into a tree or a frog. He thought of rays from outer space; that was more likely. Perhaps the Martians were doing it.

At that moment the park bell began to ring. Eric remembered the message he was going to write, and

hurried off. He left the park through the top gates and went down Church Street. On the way, it occurred to him that there was an even shorter cut he could have taken. Dogs didn't need to follow paths or roads. He could've cut across the allotments and been home now.

Then, turning once more into Apollo Road, Eric caught a sudden whiff of a most marvellous smell. It was a smell of fish and chips, chicken and mushy peas, vinegar, tomato ketchup and pineapple fritters. It was Purnell's fish shop: they had everything there. Eric hesitated, then crossed the road and went up Union Street. It was hardly out of his way. He would just take a look.

The light from Purnell's fish shop glowed into the street. Eric stood outside. A couple of older boys were sitting on a wall eating bags of chips. He recognized one of them; his name was Hopper. He was a fourth year in Mr Hodge's class. Since Raymond Fletcher had left, he was the boss of the school. The other boy was the boy on the bike who had passed Eric in the park. He was dropping chips into his mouth as though they were grapes. Eric watched in fascination. He felt his mouth watering, and had the urge to sit up and beg.

The boy caught Eric staring at him. 'You're a nosy dog,' he said. 'Hey, Hopper, look at this nosy dog!'

'Give him a chip,' said Hopper.

'You give him one!'

'No – you!'

'You!'

This went on for a while. Eric looked at one boy, then the other. It was like watching tennis. Finally, Hopper leant forward on the wall and held out a chip. Eric didn't hesitate. He loved chips. Besides, the chance to eat one of Hopper's was too good to miss. Hopper was the kind of boy who'd eat *your* chips whether you offered him any or not. Eric sat up, took the chip from Hopper's not entirely clean hand, and ate it. It was delicious. Again it had that 'different' flavour he couldn't quite find words for.

Then a man came out of the shop. He had a bottle of beer in his coat pocket and was carrying an open bag of fish and chips. 'That's a smart dog. Does he like fish?' The man broke off a piece of fish and held it out. Once more Eric did his trick: sat up, neatly took the fish, and ate it. Lovely!

'How about pineapple fritter?' said the man. He removed a separate bag (wrapped in newspaper) from his other pocket.

'I'd sit up for that!' said Hopper.

Eric ate the piece of fritter he was offered. He felt pleased with himself. For a second time it occurred to him that being a dog might not be all bad. He could make a living like this, if he had to.

But now Eric could hear and *feel* a curious thumping going on behind him. He spun round but there was nothing there. He heard it again. Again he turned, and this time found the answer. Of course, he should have guessed, it was his own tail wagging.

At this point an old woman in carpet slippers joined the group. She was wearing an apron and carrying a bottle of lemonade.

Hopper's friend said, 'Let's see if he can catch!' He tossed a chip into the air. Eric leapt, opened his

25

mouth, and to his own surprise caught it. Usually, he wasn't all that good at catching. Then Hopper threw one; but his throw was wild and Eric missed. He sniffed the chip where it lay on the pavement. It was covered with dirt; quite uneatable. He turned away and looked expectantly at Hopper.

'Got nice manners, for a dog,' said the old woman. 'Won't eat 'em off the floor, will he?'

Just then the man and the bull-mastiff that Eric had met earlier came walking up the street. Eric was reluctant to leave. He was enjoying himself. A game where you caught things and *ate* them, that was better than rounders, any day. But the mastiff was barking again, and growling too. Eric didn't hang about. He barked once himself, and hurried off the way he had come.

From Apollo Road Eric made his way up Clay Street. Shortly after he found himself outside his own house. Now he began to regret the time he had wasted. Writing a message in Emily's sand-pit was still a good idea; but the sand-pit was at the back of the house, and the side gate was locked. Also, it had become quite dark. If he were able to write, could his parents see to read? Also, all that running – climbing hills – jumping for chips, had worn him out. His little legs felt like lead.

Eric sat on his haunches and peered through a gap in the fence. As he did so, he noticed two things: one, his mum was in the garden, watering the roses; two, the front door was open! That was enough for Eric. In no time at all he had changed his plan. He would sneak into the house instead, if he could, and hide in his room. He could write the message in the morning. His chances would be better then. He could reach the back of the house. It would be light. Besides, there was the prospect of curling up on his own bed, and no bull-mastiff to bother him. With this in mind, Eric was encouraged to try his luck.

The first stage proved easy. He wriggled under the bottom rail of the fence and crept along behind the cover of the rose bushes. His mum was humming a tune and had her back to him. He reached the safety of the hall.

Then there was his dad to watch out for. But that proved easy, too. He was in the bathroom, shaving. Postmen have to get up early, and Eric's dad often shaved at night to save time in the morning. Eric crept upstairs to the landing. His bedroom door had swung to, so that it looked more or less shut. He nudged it open and went inside. The light from a street lamp shone faintly through the curtains. His pyjamas – that Eric supposed he would never wear again – still lay in a heap on the floor. He was surprised once more by how big everything looked: the huge chair with his huge clothes on it; the giant bed looming above him.

Eric gathered himself and leapt onto the bed. He turned round a few times to find a comfortable position. He put his head on his paws. The air was heavy with the smell of blanket and sheet, and Airfix glue. There was a half-finished model of a moon buggy on the dresser. He yawned. 'This is better, though if Dad looks in there'll be trouble.' He yawned again. 'I'm a dog ... a *dog*! What'll Mum say when she knows? ... What'll Roy say? "Brilliant," Roy'll say.'

Eric heard a faint sound downstairs. It was the

front door closing. He felt his eyelids growing heavy. 'Will I dream human dreams or dog dreams?' He thought about his auntie's cat, the way its whiskers twitched when *it* was dreaming. He closed his eyes.

At that moment, Eric began to feel a curious tingling in his paws. This – although he didn't know it yet – was his paws turning into hands and feet. He felt an itch around his neck. This was the fur beginning to get shorter. He felt his nose becoming warm and dry, his ears becoming flat against his head. Eric opened his eyes. He didn't move at first. The thought in his mind was: 'I'm turning back into a boy!'

But as soon as the itching and tingling stopped, he shot out of bed and pulled back the curtains. Light from the street lamp poured in. Eric felt a tremendous urge to laugh and shout. No more being thrown out of the house – his troubles were over. He was himself again. He was back!

Then, suddenly, he had another thought: he was standing there with no clothes on. What was

28

worse, he'd been running round the streets with no clothes on. *Girls* had seen him! Eric's face grew hot. Hurriedly, he drew the curtains across, grabbed his pyjamas and put them on. He got back into bed.

Gradually, after that, his embarrassment faded. It wasn't so bad when he thought about it. He'd been covered with fur, after all; and if he'd had a T-shirt and shorts on, he'd have looked sillier. Besides, nobody *knew* it was him. Eric yawned, and yawned again. There was a jumble of thoughts crowding in his head; but he was immensely weary. He turned over on his side. 'Wait till morning,' he thought. 'Wait till Roy hears...' He closed his eyes; 'Brilliant!...' and fell asleep.

4

Roy Ackerman

The next morning when Eric woke up, he was confused. His first thought was: 'Am I a boy or a dog?' and his second: 'What made me think *that*?' Then he looked at his hands. They were as dirty as he had ever seen them, but they *were* hands.

His mum entered the room and drew the curtains. 'Come on, Eric – sun's shining!'

'Mum, I want to tell you something.'

'Yes,' said his mum. She left the room. Eric heard her on the landing, talking to Emily. He raised his voice, 'Did you see a dog in the house last night?'

'Yes – did it wake you?' Mrs Banks came in again, carrying his clean shirt and socks, and followed by Emily. Emily had her dressing-gown on and her thumb in her mouth.

'Mum,' said Eric, 'I want to tell you something.'

'I saw a dog,' said Emily. 'I want one.'

Mrs Banks put Eric's clean clothes on the chair and picked up the dirty ones.

Eric got out of bed. 'You know that dog, well...'

'I want one,' said Emily.

Mrs Banks gazed round the room as though she had forgotten something. Then she looked at Eric. Then she *stared* at him.

'Mum, y'see, that dog –'

'Eric, look at your face! Didn't you wash last night?'

'Well...'

'Let me see your hands!'

Reluctantly, Eric held them out. 'About this dog...'

'I want one,' said Emily.

When Mrs Banks saw Eric's hands, she was horrified. It wasn't like him to go to bed in that condition. Eric wanted to say that the reason his hands were dirty was that last night they'd been paws and he'd been running round the streets on them. But somehow he couldn't get the words out. He thought of revealing his feet. They'd be as bad, and ought to prove something. But he couldn't bring himself to do that either. Instead he accepted the telling-off. When his mum sent him to the bathroom, he managed to keep his feet out of sight. After that, he got dressed, had his first breakfast and went off on his cousin Marion's paper-round. Maybe he could tell his mum when he returned. In any case, one thing was sure: he *could* tell Roy.

Eric collected his papers at the newsagent's. He had been doing the round for nearly three weeks now, ever since Marion had broken her arm. He

hoped to be doing it for a while yet. Marion was ready to return, but her mum said it was too soon. He set off up the road. As usual, Roy was waiting for him at the corner of Freeth Street. Roy never went to the shop. Mr Sturgess – he was the newsagent – didn't like paper-rounds to be shared.

Roy Ackerman was taller than Eric; frecklier, too. His hair was gingerish and wiry. It wouldn't lie flat, not even after swimming. On most occasions he wore a sort of jockey cap. Roy was an excitable boy. The kind of boy who rarely stopped talking in class, unless the teacher asked him a question. Mrs Jessop said he was a bad influence on Eric. Roy's mother blamed the school. She said Eric was a bad influence on *him*.

Eric and Roy had known each other since playschool. They had been friends since the infants. In Mrs Jessop's class, they sat at a table near the front. Eric sat there so that he could see the marker-board. (He was a bit short-sighted.) Roy sat there so that Mrs Jessop could see him.

'I've got something to tell you, Roy,' said Eric. 'You won't believe it, though.'

'I'll believe it,' said Roy.

'No, you won't.'

'Yes, I will.'

'You won't, Roy.'

'I will – I'll believe anything!'

'Right,' said Eric. 'Last night I turned into a dog.'

Roy paused. He was pushing a *Radio Times* through a letter-box. 'Well, *nearly* anything,' he said. And then, 'What sort of dog?'

'A Norfolk terrier,' said Eric. 'Then I went downstairs and Dad thought I was a real dog and put me out. It was half-past ten before I got back in. Then I changed into a boy again.'

For a moment Roy and Eric separated to deliver papers on opposite sides of the road. Then Eric continued: 'When I woke up, my hands and feet were black from running round the streets. You can ask my mum, she saw them – and Emily. I chased a cat!'

Roy listened closely to what Eric was saying, and

watched his face whenever he got the chance. Eric had never pulled his leg before; he wasn't that kind of boy. Roy had always admired Eric, ever since the infants. He was the one who worked things out. The one who usually made them *up* was him – Roy. All the same: 'turning into a dog', that took some believing. Roy began to make an effort to believe it. 'Did you catch the cat?' he said.

Other questions that Roy asked during the paper-round were: 'What did it feel like?', plus three or four versions of, 'Were you scared?'. When they delivered the papers in Stone Street, they encountered the bull-mastiff again. It was chained up at the back of number 16. It barked and leapt against the side gate. Its chain rattled. Eric described his meetings with the dog the night before.

'What did you do?' said Roy.

And Eric said, 'Barked at it!'

In Vicarage Road they met Eric's dad. He was out on *his* round. As usual, the two boys stopped to say hello. Mr Banks had a quick look at the sports page in one of the papers, and gave them each a mint imperial. Afterwards Roy said, 'How about your dad, does he know?'

'Nobody knows,' said Eric. 'Just me and you.'

'Didn't you tell your mum?'

Eric shook his head. 'I was going to, but I couldn't.'

'I wouldn't tell mine,' said Roy. 'She'd say I was making it up.' He pulled his jockey cap over his eyes. 'So it's a secret – just you and me!'

'Well . . . yes,' said Eric.

And Roy, who was perhaps now beginning to believe it – or *half*-believe it – said, 'Brilliant!'

From then on there was little time for talking.

They were behind with the round: it was late. As soon as they'd finished, Eric raced home for his second breakfast. Roy also went home. He said he'd call for Eric in about ten minutes.

When Eric came into the kitchen, he found his mum drinking a cup of tea. His sister was chalking a picture on her blackboard and sneaking a cornflake once in a while from Eric's bowl, where they were poured out ready. Eric sat down, added milk and sugar, and began to eat. His mum drank her tea and watched him. 'You're a bit late.'

'Yes,' said Eric.

'What was it you wanted to tell me?'

'What?' said Eric. He'd heard well enough, but was playing for time. Suddenly, he knew he wasn't going to tell his mum, not yet anyway.

'What did you want to tell me?' said his mum.

'Er ... can't remember.' Eric bent over his bowl. He could feel his mum's gaze on the back of his neck. She had a way of finding things out that was a permanent mystery to him.

Mrs Banks carried her cup to the sink and glanced out of the window. 'Are you all right, Eric?'

'Yes,' said Eric. He turned his attention to Emily. She was crouching at her blackboard with her back to him. 'What are you drawing?'

'Dog,' said Emily, without looking round.

And his mum said, 'She wants one.'

Eric finished his breakfast and found the things he needed for school: his plimsolls, a bag of cabbage stalks for the student's rabbit, and his school camp money. This was in an envelope on the table. After that, Roy arrived. He drew a hat on Emily's dog, which she thought was very funny. Eric gave him a look and a nudge. The look said: 'I haven't told my mum, and she thinks we're up to something.' Eric could see his mum was watching *Roy*. The nudge said: 'Let's go!'

On the way to school, Roy asked more questions. He'd had time to think. Although he never said it in so many words, what he was looking for now was proof. Eric realized this and did what he could. In an odd way, *he* was looking for proof, too.

'I told you about writing in the dirt, didn't I?' They were approaching the front playground.

'Yes,' said Roy. 'So we could ask that woman, y'mean.'

'*You* could ask her,' Eric said. They entered the playground. 'And I told you about begging for chips.'

Roy laughed. 'Begging for chips!' He loved that, whether it was true or not.

Ahead of them, a pile of boys were struggling on the ground. Perched on top was a familiar figure, looking pleased with himself. It was Hopper.

Eric and Roy stared at each other.

Roy said, 'Didn't you say –'

'Yes,' Eric said. 'It was Hopper! It was Hopper I got the chips off. That's the proof – ask him!'

'Right,' said Roy, then hesitated. The trouble was, asking Hopper was easier said than done. Hopper was unpredictable. He could get a gang onto you for looking at him; for *not* looking at him, even.

Hopper was a solid boy. He had a square body and a square head. He never wore a coat, even when it snowed. He had transfers of famous racing cars stuck on his arms, and tattoos in blue felt pen on the backs of his hands.

Roy took his jockey cap off and put it on again. 'You ask him,' he said.

'I don't need to ask him,' said Eric. 'I was there. You ask him!'

A red ball came bouncing towards them, followed by a pack of first-year boys. Roy kicked the ball back over their heads. 'I've got it,' he said. 'Let's get Kenny Biggs to ask him.' Kenny was Hopper's cousin; also he was in Roy and Eric's class.

So, Kenny was approached, told as little as was necessary, and promised a handful of Eric's crisps at playtime for his trouble. He agreed to do the job.

'Ask him, was he at Purnell's fish shop last night?' said Eric.

'And was there a dog there?' said Roy.

'And what happened?' Eric said.

Kenny went off in search of Hopper. He had left the pile of boys he'd been sitting on, and gone into the back playground. Eric and Roy sat on the dustbins outside the caretaker's room. The red ball came bouncing towards them again. This time Eric took a kick at it. The pursuing first years yelled in protest, turned and followed the ball. Then Kenny came back.

'What did he say?' said Roy and Eric together.

'Hopper says, "Who wants to know?",' said Kenny Biggs.

5

One Bark for 'Yes'

Roy and Eric were still considering their next move when the whistle went and put a stop to everything. The children began lining up in their classes. The teachers came out to lead them in.

Rolfe Street Primary – that was the name of the school – was old. It had tall, thin windows like a church. There were iron railings at the front and a high brick wall at the back. The headmaster was old, too; his name was Mr Blocker.

Eric and Roy lined up with Class Three facing Mrs Jessop. Roy said, 'Let's ask him again, at playtime!'

'Face the front,' said Mrs Jessop. 'Come on, Roy!'

Class Three – girls first – followed Mrs Jessop up the steps and along the corridor. The walls were covered in brown tiles to about shoulder height; so were the classroom walls.

In the classroom, the student, Mr Cork, was feeding his rabbit. Eric handed him the bag of cabbage stalks. One of the monitors wrote the date on the marker-board. Mrs Jessop called the register. 'Antony Able?'

'Here, Miss.'

'Roy Ackerman?'

'Here, Miss.'

'Dennis Ball?'

'Gone to the dentist, Miss!'

'No – I saw him playing out!'

'His sister says –'

'Sh!' said Mrs Jessop. 'Eric Banks?'

'Here, Miss.'

'Woof!'

Mrs Jessop glared. 'Who did that? Was it you, Roy?'

'No, Miss!' said Roy. He had barked quite softly, intending – or maybe *half*-intending – only Eric to hear.

Mrs Jessop completed the register and did the dinner register. The children with school camp money took it down the corridor to Mr Hodge. The bell went for assembly. During assembly, Mr Blocker talked about how Jesus loved the little children and suffered them to come unto Him. He talked about some boys who'd been having a spitting competition in the back playground. He warned what would happen if they did it again.

Roy and Eric talked about Hopper. Roy was worried. He felt sure Hopper had been giving him a look when he, Hopper, came into assembly. After assembly, Class Three had a maths lesson with Mr Cork. He gave them work cards, one between two. They had to measure various things and calculate their surface areas. Then it was playtime.

Eric bought a bag of crisps from the fourth-year shop. He and Roy kicked a ball around with Tony Able. Kenny – bribed with crisps – went looking for Hopper.

'Tell him it's for a bet or something,' said Roy. 'Give him a crisp.'

But this time all went well. Perhaps Hopper was in a good mood. He was unpredictable in more ways than one. He did unpredictable favours sometimes. Whatever the reason, when Kenny came back, he had the information. 'Hopper says, yes – he was at Purnell's – it was after ten o'clock.'

'See, I told you,' said Eric, looking at Roy.

'He says there *was* a dog, and him and Martin Smart had it jumping for chips.'

'See?' said Eric.

'They had it jumping for fish and pineapple fritters, too, Hopper says.'

Well, that settled it for Roy. He couldn't believe it, but he *did* believe it. The idea that Eric himself might have gone to Purnell's fish shop and seen a real dog begging for chips, and made the rest of it up, never occurred to him; or if it did, he dismissed it. Eric wouldn't do a thing like that. Eric, for his part, was relieved. He'd begun to have doubts himself. For some reason, it seemed better to know he'd turned into a dog – to have it *proved* – than to find out he'd imagined it.

Eric gave Kenny the rest of his crisps. Tony Able sneaked out of the gates to fetch his ball. Once more Eric and Roy sat on the dustbins. Roy was excited. He took his jockey cap off and put it on again three or four times, and when Kenny left, he punched the flat of his hand with his fist. 'It's brilliant, Eric – you really turned into a dog!'

'I told you,' said Eric.

'Yes, but you really did!' Roy stood on a dustbin and jumped up and down.

Just then, a man's face with a frown on it appeared at the window behind them. It was Mr Moody, the caretaker. He knocked on the window and gestured for Roy to get down from the dustbin. He mouthed a single word through the glass: 'Off!'

After play Class Three watched a TV programme in the hall with Mr Cork. It was about the various animals that could be found on the banks of a river. Roy stared in the direction of the set, but saw very little. He talked to Eric out of the side of his mouth. 'I've been thinking – if you changed once, you could change again.'

'I know,' said Eric.

'You could change any time.'

'Yes.'

Mr Cork tapped Eric on the head with a TV pamphlet. 'Watch the programme,' he said.

On the way back to the classroom Eric said, 'Listen – if I *do* change, we'll need a code.'

'A code!' Roy stopped and looked admiringly at Eric. 'Hey, that's good!' The children behind protested. They wanted to get into the classroom and Roy was blocking the door.

Roy and Eric sat down. Mr Cork began to ask questions about the programme. 'So this is it,' said Eric. 'One bark for "yes"; two barks for "no".'

'Right,' said Roy. 'One for yes, two for no.' He muttered the formula to himself two or three times. Then he thought of something else. 'What shall I call you, if you're a dog?'

'It was a vole, Sir,' said Eric.

Roy blinked. Mr Cork must have asked Eric a question. Roy couldn't have answered it. He'd forgotten Mr Cork was even there. He said again, 'What shall I call you?'

'Eric,' said Eric.

'That's no name for a dog. How about . . . Rex?'

'No,' said Eric. 'Call me Eric.'

At dinner time Eric and Roy sat at the same table. The servers were two girls from Class Three: Joan Spooner and Alison Jukes. Eric and Roy liked it on their table. The girls didn't eat much themselves, and gave big helpings. On some of the fourth-year tables, you were lucky even to smell a dinner.

The teacher on duty was Mr Hodge. He stood on the platform and folded his arms. 'Hands together, eyes closed!'

Roy said, 'I've just thought of something!'

'You, too, Roy!' said Mr Hodge.

Roy lowered his head and squinted sideways at Eric.

'For what we are about to receive,' said Mr Hodge. The children took up the words. 'For what we are

43

about to receive may the Lord make us truly thankful Amen.'

Roy said, 'Listen – if you were a dog, you'd have to buy a licence – $37\frac{1}{2}$p!'

'Servers!' said Mr Hodge. Joan and Alison hurried up to the hatch.

'No,' Eric said. 'You need a licence to *have* a dog, not *be* one. Dogs don't buy them.'

The dinner was shepherd's pie, peas and gravy; the pudding: treacle tart and custard.

'Just think, you could be eating bonemeal biscuits and Pedigree Chum,' said Roy.

'What's all this about dogs?' said Joan.

'Who says? I had pineapple fritter last time.'

'What's all this about dogs?' said Alison.

'It's a secret – isn't it, Eric?'

Eric poured himself a glass of water. 'Woof!' he said.

In the afternoon Class Three put on their plimsolls and went into the hall for a square-dancing lesson with Mrs Jessop. Eric managed fairly well, but Roy had trouble concentrating. Mrs Jessop was in a cheerful mood. She had her plimsolls on and joined in the dancing. She clapped her hands to the music. But towards the end, Roy's behaviour exasperated her and she threw a bean-bag at him.

For the last lesson of the day Mrs Jessop took the slow readers in the staffroom. Mr Cork read the rest of the class a story. From time to time there were interruptions: two girls with a message for the netball team; two girls with items of lost property; one infant with a worried look on his face; he'd come to the wrong room.

It was hot in the classroom. The children were

warm, too, from dancing. They daydreamed in their places while the story floated in the air around them. Even Roy was still. Then Mrs Jessop returned with the readers and the bell went for home-time.

The children put the chairs up on the tables.

'Good afternoon, Class Three!' said Mrs Jessop.

'Good afternoon, Mrs Jessop, good afternoon, Mr Cork!' the children said, and filed out.

6

Be My Dog

Eric and Roy walked home. They crossed Rolfe Street at the school crossing. Roy said, 'About this code, I've been thinking, why not nod your head for "yes" and shake it for "no"?'

'I prefer to bark,' said Eric.

'Or sometimes you could write.'

'I'll bark,' Eric said.

In Seymour Road the two boys bought a liquorice wheel and a liquorice pipe from Russell's sweet shop.

'Another thing,' said Roy, 'if you change again, I want you to come round.'

'What if it's late? You'll be in bed.'

'I want you to come,' said Roy. 'You could howl at the window.'

Eric and Roy balanced along the wall in front of the Old People's Home. They watched a fire-engine going up Joining's Bank. 'Dogs chase fire-engines, y'know,' said Roy. And he said, 'If you *do* change, you might not change back – think of that!'

'I already did,' said Eric.

'Well, the thing is,' Roy threw his jockey cap in the air and caught it; 'what I was thinking was – you could be *my* dog.'

'Thanks,' said Eric.

'Yes. I'd get my Uncle Colin to make you a kennel.'

'I'd rather live in the house,' said Eric.

They passed a postbox. Roy pushed his arm inside as far as it would go. 'I always wanted a dog,' he said.

On most evenings after school Roy and Eric would have their tea and go to the park. But Thursday was Roy's staying-in night. He had a piano lesson at half-past four, and had to practise afterwards.

Roy and Eric separated at the junction of Clay Street and Taylors Road. Roy was hopping with frustration. He couldn't bear to let Eric out of his sight. If he was going to turn into a dog again, Roy wanted to be there. All the same, what could he do? If he missed his lesson, his mum would keep him in for a week – well, a few days, anyway. She'd done it before.

Roy walked backwards up Taylors Road. He cupped his hands to his mouth. 'Don't forget – come round!'

'Right!' said Eric.

'Come round!'

'I heard you!'

Roy kept his gaze on Eric till there was nothing to see. He pushed both hands in his pockets and continued up the road.

When Eric entered the kitchen, his dad was there. He was drinking a mug of tea and reading the *Radio Times*. His hair was tousled, and he had a sleepy look on his face. Eric's dad usually took a nap in the afternoon. This was because he started work at four o'clock in the morning.

'Your mouth's all black,' he said.

'I've been eating a liquorice wheel,' said Eric.

He looked out of the window. His mum was unpegging washing from the line. Emily was playing with her play-pool. She had her swimming costume on, and was fetching things from all over the garden and putting them in the water. Mrs Banks came in with the basket of washing.

'Your mouth's black,' she said.

'I've been eating liquorice,' said Eric.

He went into the garden and looked in Emily's pool. It was full of leaves and flower-heads. Two of her little plastic dolls were in there, and a dinosaur, and a driver from one of his cars.

'Mouth's black,' said Emily.

'Liquorice,' said Eric. He gave Emily the bit he had saved for her. When she wasn't looking, he rescued his driver from the pool.

Eric returned to the house and went up to his room. He came down and went into the garden again. He was restless. His head was full of uncomfortable thoughts. Without Roy to talk to, he had trouble sorting them out. Also, everything was – well – *funnier* when Roy was around.

'What if I change *now*!' he thought. 'At teatime! What if I only half change, or they put me out and that mastiff gets me!'

Eric had another problem, too. His mum was watching him again. The longer he didn't tell her anything, the more of a secret it became, and the more he felt suspected. When they were having tea, Mr Banks said, 'Did you tell Eric about that dog?'

'Yes, he heard it – didn't you, Eric?'

'Yes,' said Eric.

'Strange,' said Mr Banks. 'I thought I knew all the dogs round here.'

Some time later Mrs Banks leant over the table

and placed a hand on Eric's forehead. 'Does he look all right to you, Charles?'

'He looks all right,' said Mr Banks. 'A bit ugly, maybe.'

'Charles!' Mrs Banks laughed. Eric laughed too; so did Emily. Emily hadn't got the joke; she was laughing because everyone else was. Then the others laughed because she was laughing. Emily laughed the more. A piece of tomato shot out of her mouth and fell in the butter.

After tea Eric watched television for a while. His dad had gone to the sorting office to do some overtime. His mum was bathing Emily. Eric switched from one channel to the next. Finally, he switched off altogether and tried to read a book. But it was no use; he couldn't concentrate. He put the book down and stared at himself in the sideboard mirror.

Suddenly, out of the corner of his eye, he caught a slight movement which made him jump. He turned in time to see a face at the window with hands cupped round it, peering in. It was Roy.

Eric opened the window.

'Can't stop,' said Roy. 'Just sneaked out.' He glanced into the room. 'Where is everybody?'

Eric told him.

Roy said, 'I've been thinking – what if you only half changed?'

'*I* thought of that,' said Eric.

'The thing is, what would you rather be: a boy with a dog's head, or a dog with a boy's head?'

While Eric was considering this, his mum came into the room. 'Hello, Roy!'

'Hello, Mrs Banks,' said Roy.

Eric – with his back to his mum – gave Roy a look. The look said: 'Be careful what you say.'

Roy cleared his throat. He took his jockey cap off and twirled it on his finger.

'Isn't Roy coming in?' said Mrs Banks.

'Aren't you coming in?' said Eric.

'No,' said Roy. 'I've got to go – just sneaked, er . . . *came* out, y'know.' He gave Eric a look. The look said: 'Don't forget – come round!' And then he left.

Mrs Banks put the television on. She sat down on the sofa with a bag of wool. 'Is *Roy* all right?' she said.

7

St Mary's Baths

The next morning when Eric woke up he was still a boy. As usual he met Roy on the paper round.

Roy said, 'Maybe it'll only happen at special times, like Midsummer's Eve, or Wednesdays.'

'I thought of that,' said Eric.

On the way to school Roy proposed another theory. 'Perhaps it'll only happen in your own bed.'

'What makes you think that?' said Eric.

'Well, Dad told me this story once, called "Jimmy and His Magic Patch". It was in a comic he used to read. Y'see, this boy has a magic patch on his trousers. It comes from a magician's carpet or something. And every now and then it flies off with him to different places. Then he has adventures there.'

'What's that got to do with my bed?' said Eric.

'Well, I was thinking: what kind of blankets have you got?'

When they entered the playground, Kenny Biggs was waiting for them.

'Where's your swimming things?' said Eric. The three of them had arranged to go swimming straight after school.

'Can't go,' said Kenny. 'Mum's having her hair done. I've got to mind Malky.'

Roy said, 'Hey, look at Hopper!' Hopper was on the boilerhouse roof, which was, of course, forbidden. He was getting a ball.

Kenny said, 'D'you want me to ask him anything? I can if you want.'

'No,' said Eric.

'Oh,' said Kenny. He looked disappointed. He was hoping for more crisps.

During assembly Roy tried to talk to Eric about another idea he'd had; but Mrs Jessop heard him and made him stand at the side. At playtime they helped Mr Cork to move some tables and clear a space for the drama lesson. Joan Spooner and Alison Jukes asked them to be in their play.

'Alison wants you to be in our play,' said Joan.

'No, *she* wants you to,' said Alison.

At dinner-time a dog got into the playground. It was large and friendly. It ran around and joined in various games. About thirty children tried to help

53

the dinner ladies to catch it. About a dozen said they knew the dog and where it lived. They volunteered to take it home. Roy and Eric sat on the dustbins and watched the chase. 'Just think,' said Roy. 'That could be you.'

When home-time came, the children going on the school camp were given a letter and a list. The letter was about a meeting for the parents. The list was all the things the children needed to take with them. Eric and Roy read theirs on the way to the swimming baths.

Roy said, 'It says here, "Four pairs of socks". Who needs four pairs of socks?'

'"Comfortable walking boots",' said Eric.

'"Stamped-addressed postcard",' said Roy.

'"Pocket-money",' said Eric. 'Hey, look at this: "No more than £1"!'

They were in the High Street now. The wool shop where Mrs Banks had a part-time job was close by. Friday was one of her days.

'A pound? I need more than that,' said Roy.

'It's in a field, y'know. You can't spend money in a field.'

They had reached the baths and were climbing the front steps.

'There'll be shops,' said Roy. 'I want to buy presents.'

Eric and Roy paid their money and got changed. The cubicles were in a row along the side of the bath. There was a similar row on the other side for girls and women. Each cubicle had a bench seat, two wall-hooks and a sliding plastic curtain, like a shower curtain. Eric and Roy put their clothes in the metal baskets and handed them in. They were given rubber rings with numbers on them to wear round their wrists. They washed their feet in the footbath.

Eric stepped up to the pool and dived straight in. Roy stood on the side for a while, winding himself up. Eric was the better swimmer; he had his grade two. Roy didn't have grade one yet. He'd only learnt to swim since Easter.

'What's it like?' said Roy.

'Boiling!' said Eric. 'Come on in!'

Roy swung his arms a couple of times, jumped in and began to swim across the bath. His eyes were shut. He moved through the water like a thrashing machine. He seemed to be swimming for his life.

Roy reached Eric and opened his eyes. 'This is great!' he said.

After that the two boys spent their time playing games, most of which seemed to involve jumping in, climbing up the steps and jumping in again. Roy shouted, 'Bombs away!' and 'Geronimo!'. Eric swung into the water on an imaginary rope and made Tarzan calls. The attendant told them to keep the noise down. Later, Eric showed Roy how to stand on his hands. He tried it, but the water went up his nose. Roy challenged Eric to a race. Eric may have been the better swimmer, but Roy – over short distances – was faster. Eventually, after about forty minutes, the attendant wrote some numbers on a board and blew his whistle. The numbers included Roy's and Eric's. It was time to leave.

Roy and Eric went to the clothes store and collected their baskets. They found a pair of unoccupied cubicles. They began to get changed. Eric stood with his wet trunks round his ankles and dried himself. The towel was rough and had a freshly laundered smell. It reminded him of sitting on his dad's knee when he was small, having his hair dried. On the other side of the partition Roy was singing.

Eric reached for his T-shirt ... and then it happened. There was a sudden itch between his shoulders, a curious tingling in his hands and feet, a *shrinking* feeling in every part of him (except his ears), and a sensation in his stomach like going over a hump-back bridge in a car. At last, in hardly more than fifteen seconds, the transformation was complete. Eric, the boy, had disappeared; Eric, the dog, had arrived.

8

Exit Eric

When Roy saw a dog's head poke under the partition, he stopped singing. When the dog joined him in the cubicle and he could see it was a Norfolk terrier, he said, 'A dog! I don't believe it! Eric – is that you?'

Somehow Eric kept his wits and remembered the code. 'Woof!' he said.

Roy, for his part, was immediately confused. He was scared (a little) and excited (a lot). '"Woof"?' he said. 'What's that, one for yes . . . ?'

'Woof!' said Eric.

'. . . or one for no?'

'Woof, woof!' Eric said.

But already Roy was hardly listening. He couldn't concentrate on codes. Instead he crouched and peered intently into Eric's face. 'Eric? I think I recognize you, Eric. You've got the *same* expression.'

Now Roy was looking under the partition into Eric's cubicle. He could see a pair of feet in the next-but-one, but Eric's was empty. His excitement grew. 'It is you, isn't it? It's really happened!' Then, almost without thinking, he patted his friend's head and ruffled the fur along his back. 'Hey, this is great, Eric – it's brilliant!' (The truth is, Roy had been waiting for Eric to change ever since he'd known it was possible. He'd even felt irritated at times because it was taking so long. He almost accused Eric of not trying.)

Eric sat on the floor avoiding the puddles and Roy's wet trunks. He looked up at Roy, who was the picture of a contented swimmer: puckered face, red-rimmed eyes, and – especially in his case – cockatoo hair. He had his underpants on and one sock.

Eric, of course, couldn't altogether share Roy's opinion. When the transformation began he'd briefly felt more frantic than the first time. This time he knew what was coming! Now – having recovered somewhat, and being the level-headed boy he was – the thought in his mind was: How do I get out of here? Also, he was beginning to feel concerned about his clothes, his swimming kit, his bag, his watch, and his crisp and lolly money. And the question was: How reliable was Roy?

Eric had a high regard for Roy. He was his best friend; the *best* best friend he'd ever had. Yes, Roy would stick by him, that wasn't the problem. The problem was, would he be any *use*? Roy was never short of ideas, but his brain was like a Catherine wheel; it threw them off in all directions.

Roy, meanwhile, was pulling on his other sock and talking more or less non-stop. 'How're you feeling, Eric? What's it like down there? So much for Jimmy and His Magic Patch, hey?'

When he'd finished dressing, he quickly squeezed his trunks out and rolled them up in his towel. Then he put the towel and trunks in his bag and sat on the bench. Then he said, 'Right!' and clapped his hands. Then he leapt up, took his jockey cap from its hook on the wall, and sat down again. Then he said, 'Right!' again. Then he put his jockey cap on. Then he took it off. Finally, he put his elbows on his knees, his chin in his cupped hands and stared down at Eric ... expectantly.

Eric stared back. 'Here's trouble for a start,' he thought. 'He's waiting for *me*!' (Roy usually did wait for Eric. He wasn't the leader exactly, but he did tend to organize things.) Luckily, on this occasion, Roy was beginning to appreciate that something else was needed. 'Right!' he said, and clapped his hands. 'Let's think!'

Roy then, at great speed, thought of (and talked about) practically everything: Eric's clothes, kit, watch, money; how to get past the attendants; where to go afterwards. He even remembered the code. In reply, Eric managed a 'woof' or a 'woof, woof' now and then, but to little effect. The trouble was, 'yes' and 'no' were not much use when the questions were 'either/or': Shall we sneak you out or make a run for it? Hide you under a towel or in a bag? Smokey bacon or salt and vinegar? My house or yours?

Eric was a patient boy, and – as it turned out – a patient dog. However, there were limits. At last, when they were still in the cubicle and obviously getting nowhere, Eric gave way to a burst of serious barking; not 'woof' or 'woof, woof', but 'WOOF WOOF WOOF WOOF WOOF!'

Roy was suitably startled and his attention caught. He crouched beside his friend. 'What's up, Eric? Are you trying to tell me something or –'

'Grr!' growled Eric, and startled even himself. He hadn't thought of growling, it just came out.

Roy clutched at his jockey cap and backed away. '*Eric*?' he said. And then, 'You still there?'

At that moment something else happened. The plastic curtain was pulled aside, light flooded in, and a voice said, 'What's all this?'

Eric, it seemed, had caught more than Roy's attention.

'What's all this?' (It was the attendant, of course.) 'That your dog?'

Rapidly Eric retreated under the bench, flattened his ears and looked guilty.

'Er . . . well,' said Roy. He looked guilty, too.

'It's not allowed, y'know – no dogs!'

Now, obviously, at this point, if the attendant had simply asked Eric to leave, he would have left. In fact, he'd probably have made a more orderly exit than he usually did. After all, he didn't want any trouble; he had enough as it was. However, the attendant wasn't to know this. 'Come here!' he said, and – brushing Roy aside – he entered the cubicle and made a grab for Eric.

'I'll get him for you, Sir!' said Roy. (The 'Sir' was conscious flattery.) 'He'll come with me!'

But it was too late; Eric was on the run. First he darted under the partition back into his own cubicle. Then, when the attendant showed up there, he kept going – into the next cubicle, and the next, and the next. Some were occupied, but there was little protest. Eric was in and out so fast he was hardly

seen. At the end of the row he emerged, and – on an impulse – ran into the clothes store. This was a mistake. The attendant at his heels yelled, 'Albert – grab that dog!' Whereupon a second attendant leapt from a chair, swigged back a mug of tea, and joined the chase.

Roy, meanwhile, was struggling to catch up. He was hampered by the two bags he was carrying.

With some presence of mind, he'd thought to gather up Eric's things and bring them along.

The chase continued; in and out of the racks of clothes, then out and down a corridor into a part of the baths that Eric had never seen before. It was his extra-bad luck that the attendants were young and fit, and – what was worse – bored. When they could've been expected to give up, they didn't. This was *entertainment* for them; more fun than clothes baskets, anyway.

The corridor Eric was in had doors leading off to left and right, all of which were shut. Behind him he could hear the pounding feet of the attendants, and behind them – some way behind – Roy: 'I'm here, Eric – I'm with you!'

Suddenly, up ahead, Eric found more trouble. A woman in a white overall and carrying a pile of towels was coming towards him. Voices behind yelled, 'Joyce!' and, 'Stop that dog!' Eric skidded to a halt. She was a wide woman and it was a narrow corridor; he didn't fancy his chances. He barked a couple of times, without conviction. His pursuers closed in.

Then, when all seemed lost, a door opened and a pink man, with a towel round his middle and a paperback book in his hand, stuck his head out. 'What's this?' he said. 'Can't a bloke have a quiet bath in here?'

As the attendants tried to pacify the man, Eric saw his opportunity and darted past them, back the way he had come. Along the corridor he met up with Roy. Roy was too breathless to say much, just 'Eric!', and – a gasp or two later – 'Got your bag!' Then, together – and with the attendants chasing them

62

again — they ran back into the clothes store, out into the foyer, past the ticket kiosk and the crisp and sweet machines, through the glass doors, down the flight of broad steps — to safety.

9

The High Street

Roy, with a swimming bag on each shoulder and a
Norfolk terrier at his heel, made his way up the
High Street. His earlier feeling of guilt had faded;
now, if anything, he was indignant. 'They had no
business doing that!'

'Woof!' agreed Eric.

'You weren't no trouble.'

'Woof!'

'*And* you'd paid!'

When they were well clear of the baths, Roy
stopped, took out his towel and gave his hair a rub.
Then he combed his hair using a shop window as a
mirror. Then he said, 'Hey, perhaps that's it —
rubbing! Like Aladdin's lamp.'

Eric made no reply. He was reading a manhole
cover which had caught his attention. 'DA/W
G.P.O. 71/No. 5' it said, whatever that meant.
Around them on the pavement, people were passing;
going home from work or school or the shops. The
road was crowded with cars and buses and bikes.
Overhead the sun was shining and there was a
warm breeze. It was about five o'clock.

Roy shouldered his bags and continued up the
street. Habit was taking charge: it was the route
they usually took. Eric followed. Already he was

finding that the role of well-trained dog came natur-
ally to him. Besides, it was safer just behind Roy;
less chance of being hit by a pram, for instance,
which was a hazard like a tank for a dog his size.
Roy glanced back now and then to check where Eric
was. When they came to a T-junction and Eric sat
quietly at his heel, Roy looked about to see if
passers-by were noticing; admiring Eric, admiring
him for the talented dog-handler he so obviously
was. Roy felt delighted and guilty (again) for being
delighted. 'Poor Eric,' he thought; and, 'This is
great!'

Roy had other thoughts too, such as, 'Who'd
believe it? It's like U.F.O.s. I've seen U.F.O.s, I've
seen loads.' Roy, of course, *did* believe it. With the

evidence of his own eyes, he was long past the stage of needing proof. 'I thought I believed it before,' he thought. 'Now I double believe it.'

Eric, for his part, was thinking about feet, and the immense variety of things worn on them: shoes and sandals, plimsolls and flip-flops, wellingtons even – on a day like this! Down in the moving forest of legs in which he found himself, feet were all-important. There was the constant risk of being trodden on, the occasional smell of unwashed socks and the swirling dust, which already once or twice had made him sneeze. The dust had the further effect of increasing his thirst. He was always thirsty after swimming, anyway. He thought of the ice lollies he and Roy usually bought on the way home, and wondered if Roy would think of them. Then he thought of his tea (he was hungry, too), and his mum and dad, and Emily, and what was he going to do, and where was he going to go, and things like that.

As it turned out, twenty yards away, across the street in the wool shop, Mrs Banks was thinking of Eric. She had just happened to look out as Roy went by. She waved and tapped the window, but he was too absorbed to see her, and Eric, of course, was too low. Mrs Banks was puzzled. It *was* Roy, wasn't it? But where was Eric, and was that *two* bags Roy was carrying? Also there was the dog that seemed to be following Roy...

Eric, meanwhile, had reached a decision. This street was no place for him; the place for him was the park. It would be quieter there; there'd be the chance to think things out, grass to walk on, and fewer feet.

Roy had stopped to look in a television shop

window – there was a tennis match on – and swop his bags over. They were the one snag for him. 'You should've been a Great Dane, Eric,' he said. 'You could've carried me!'

Eric pranced about for a little while, unable to see the tennis and eager to leave. Finally, he set off on his own. 'Let *him* follow for a change,' he thought.

Immediately, Roy began struggling with his bags. 'Hang on, Eric – where we going?'

Eric approached the zebra crossing and sat waiting for the traffic to stop. When it did, he took a quick look left and right, cocked his head on one side to listen for traffic, and crossed the road. Roy came running after.

Just then a large woman in a green van put her head out of the passenger-side window and peered at Eric. He heard her say: 'It's that dog again!'

'What dog?' said the driver.

'Using the zebra, the one that was writing.'

'Where is he?'

'Looked left and right he did.'

'Where is he?'

The crossing was clear now and the van had begun to move away. The woman looked back over her shoulder. 'He's gone,' she said.

And the driver said, 'Geroff!'

10

The Park

By a quarter past five Eric and Roy were in the park, on the grass, beside the pond, licking ice lollies. Eric's lolly was laid out on its wrapper so he could reach it. It was his favourite flavour, lemon and lime. Roy, without too much 'either/or' this time, had bought the lollies from the ice-cream van at the park gates.

Eric licked the cool, delicious lolly with his rough tongue. It tended to slide around and he was obliged to steady it with his paw. Roy lay on his side crunching *his* lolly and watching Eric. 'This is good,' he thought. (Despite trailing Eric most of the way, he was somehow under the impression that coming to the park was *his* idea.) Suddenly, Eric's lolly skidded from its wrapper. He nosed it back, but by now there were bits of grass stuck to it. Eric considered the problem, then looked pointedly at Roy and then at the lolly. He repeated this a couple of times until Roy got the message and removed the grass.

'Dogs eat grass, y'know,' said Roy.

When he had finished his lolly, Roy put his jockey cap on Eric to see how he looked. Eric shook it off. Roy got to his feet and began swinging from the branch of a nearby tree. He gazed about. The park was fairly empty. However, on the opposite side of the pond two girls and their dog were playing with a ball. The dog was leaping around and racing back and forth between them. Roy glanced down at *his* dog and for the first time felt a twinge of discontent. Eric was still sitting there, licking away and looking thoughtful. It was bad enough that he always made his lolly last the longest when he was a boy, but to do it as a dog!

Meanwhile, Eric, being Eric, was beginning to make plans. The thoughts in his mind were: How long will it last this time? When will I change back? And (most worryingly, of course) where? If they stayed in the park he could always hide in the bushes and get dressed there. But what about Roy – and Roy's tea – and Roy's mum?

Roy, however, wasn't thinking about his tea or his mum. 'Come on, Eric, dogs are supposed to wolf things up!' Whereupon Eric did eat up, but in his own time. He proceeded to wipe one slightly sticky paw on the grass. He remained thoughtful.

Roy's exasperation grew. 'Tear about a bit,' he said. 'It *is* a park, y'know.' He tossed his jockey cap

in the air and caught it on his head. 'Here – jump
this bench!' Roy gestured towards a park bench, and,
in case Eric hadn't got the idea, jumped it himself.
'See – easy!'

Eric trotted up to the bench, climbed onto it and
sat down. He meant it as a joke, but Roy took it
badly. He pushed his hands in his pockets and
kicked moodily at a plastic cup which lay on the
ground near a litter-bin. Then, after a while, he
began to dribble with the cup around the bench. And
he said, 'Come on – tackle me!'

This time Eric didn't wait, but took up the chal-
lenge. He leapt from the bench, chased after Roy,
and made a grab for the cup. Roy eluded him. Eric
grabbed again; again Roy slipped past. Eric held off,
jockeying for position, waiting his chance. Roy
showed neat footwork and began a commentary.
'Now it's Kenny Dalglish coming through the

middle ... only Alvin Martin to beat ...' Eric darted in, grabbed the cup in his mouth and scampered off.

Then it was Roy's turn to chase and Eric's to dodge about. As soon as Roy discovered it was hard work getting even close to Eric, 'Dalglish' was substituted and 'Shilton' took his place. 'And it's an open goal ... the crowd's going mad ... only the keeper to beat.'

Roy now proceeded to hurl himself around in a series of desperate saves at the striker's feet. He grazed an elbow and a knee but hardly noticed. Eventually, with Eric nowhere near him at the time, Roy gave a leap of pure animal spirits. (Sometimes, even under normal circumstances, the difference between boys and dogs is not great.) Roy tumbled over and over on the grass. He hadn't had fun like this for days; neither had Eric. In fact, for the moment, the two friends had quite forgotten the situation they were in. They were just a fairly wild boy and a rather civilized dog, fooling around.

Then, suddenly, with Eric off his guard, Roy lunged forward and swept up ball and player in a rugby tackle.

'Foul!' yelled Eric, or rather, as it turned out, 'Woof!'

Then Roy did a lap of honour – 'This is a cup match, Eric' – with the cup itself held high. Then something else happened. A child's pedal car came into sight from the direction of the park gates. It was bright red with a Mickey Mouse face on the front. A small irate boy was running after it – and the driver was Hopper.

The small boy – who was, of course, the owner of the car – was Malcolm Biggs, Kenny's little brother. Behind him came Kenny himself and four or five other boys. They were carrying items of cricket gear: bat, batting gloves, pad, wickets, bails – and tossing a ball between them.

Hopper came to a halt. His face was flushed; it was hard work pedalling. Malcolm Biggs – usually known as Malky – was frowning, but not crying. He tugged at his brother's T-shirt and pointed at the car: 'My, my!' Malky was two and a half and well able to say 'mine'. (Being the brother of Kenny, it was his first word.) However, in moments of stress his sense of grammar often deserted him and 'my' was the most he could manage.

Kenny looked down at Hopper's solid body jammed into the little car. He did what he could. 'Come on, Hopper, you'll make him cry. You'll break it!'

Hopper stayed where he was and considered his

options: what sort of mood was he in, hostile or friendly? Then, up ahead he noticed Roy, and Roy's *two* bags, and Roy's . . . dog.

Hopper's arrival had broken the spell for Roy and Eric. Eric had immediately recalled his plight; Roy had immediately looked at his watch (he was late for tea), and the grass stains on his shirt (what would his mum say?). He picked up the bags and began to slink off. He had no need to speak to Eric; he was slinking off, too. It was the normal Rolfe Street Primary response: when Hopper arrived, you left, if you could.

Hopper, however, had other ideas. 'Hey, Ackerman, come here!'

Reluctantly, Roy turned and approached Hopper. Eric followed.

'What's all this? Them your bags? Where's Banks?'

'Carrying his mum's shopping,' said Roy. 'He just—'

But Hopper hadn't finished yet; his main questions were still to come. 'This your dog?'

'Er . . . no,' said Roy.

'It's the one you was asking about.'

'Yes.'

'Outside the fish shop.'

'Yes.'

'And it's not yours?'

'No. He sort of . . . followed me.' Roy, ill-at-ease, lowered the bags to the ground and stood twiddling with his cap. Eric did his best to look as though he had just followed Roy. Hopper looked suspicious.

Then Malky – distracted for a time – took up again his plaintive cry: 'My, my!'

And Kenny said, 'Come on, Hopper!'

And Hopper, to the dismay of Roy and Eric and the delight of Malky, climbed out of the car.

Then Malky climbed in – beaming at once – and pedalled off.

And Hopper said, 'I know this dog.'

The next few minutes were an uncomfortable period for Roy and Eric. Hopper was suddenly keen to show off what Eric could do. 'He's a smart 'un!' He looked around for something to throw. 'Give us a bail, Dobbo!'

'No,' said Dobbo, otherwise Philip Dobson, the owner of the bails and most of the gear except the bat. He and another boy were pacing out the pitch and knocking in the stumps.

'Give us a bail!'

When the bail was handed over, Hopper said, 'Watch this, Kenny,' and tossed it towards Eric. 'Catch!'

Eric made no move except to raise his head and watch the bail disdainfully, and see it fall.

'Pretty good,' said Kenny.

Hopper tried again. Again Eric failed to move. '*You* catch it,' he thought.

Kenny had a whispered word with Roy. '*Is* it your dog?'

'Yes and no,' said Roy.

'And where *is* Eric?'

Roy shrugged his shoulders. 'Hard to say,' he said.

Hopper, meanwhile, had become displeased. 'What's all this?' He looked accusingly at Roy. 'What you been doing to this dog?'

'Er ... nothing,' said Roy. He knelt down and pretended to tie his shoelace. 'Catch it, Eric. Hopper's gonna beat me up!'

74

Fortunately, by this time the demands of the game were beginning to take Hopper's attention. The stumps were in-and Clive Smart was taking guard; it was his bat.

'I'll bowl!' said Hopper.

At which point, Roy seized his chance. In a sudden burst of over-acting, he stared wildly at his watch, said, 'Is that the time?', grabbed the bags and scurried off. Eric followed.

'Hang about!' said Hopper, but it was a half-hearted demand. His suspicions were still aroused, but he also wanted to bowl. Eric and Roy kept going. At high speed they made their way around the pond, meaning to leave by the top gates. Roy suffered in silence the banging of the bags against his ribs. Eric ignored the urge to bark at the ducks as he went by.

When they were well clear, Roy paused for breath and to swop the bags over. 'Listen – let's go to my house – I'll sneak you in.'

'Woof!' agreed Eric. He'd thought of that, too. It was the best solution.

Roy shouldered the bags again and glanced back at the cricketers. Clive Smart, it seemed, was out. Hopper was taking guard. It looked like being a long game. Hopper, of course, was not the easiest batsman to dismiss.

11

Roy's Room

When Eric and Roy came out through the park gates, they almost collided with a girl who was riding her bike on the pavement. It was Joan Spooner.

'Hello, Roy!' said Joan.

'Hello,' said Roy. 'Can't stop!' And he didn't; neither did Eric.

Joan hesitated, then turned her bike and rode after them. 'That your dog?' she called out.

'No,' said Roy, and he laughed. 'It's Eric's!'

Joan came up alongside them. She noted the bags Roy was carrying and the well-trained way the dog was following him. 'Where *is* Eric?'

'He's around somewhere,' said Roy. He stopped and waited at a set of traffic lights.

'What're you laughing at?' said Joan.

Roy said, 'What're *you* asking about Eric for?' And then, 'He's your boyfriend, that's why.'

'No, he isn't,' said Joan.

Meanwhile, Eric sat listening with a mixture of embarrassment and curiosity. Of course, he knew who Joan's boyfriend was. It was Roy.

After that the lights changed and Roy and Eric continued on their way; and Joan – somewhat puzzled – continued on hers.

As they approached Roy's house, Roy began to make elaborate plans for getting Eric past his mum and up to his room. But when he came to the back door – with Eric hiding in the garage – it was locked. And when he took the key from its usual place (under the mat) and entered the kitchen, a note on the table said, 'Gone to Mrs Turner's – back soon'. Mrs Turner was a pensioner who lived a few doors away. Roy's mum did her shopping now and then.

Roy moved swiftly, fetched Eric from the garage and hurried him upstairs. It's an odd fact that, as a boy, Eric had hardly ever been in Roy's house, and never at all in Roy's room. Roy's mother didn't encourage him to bring his friends home. She was a tidy woman. She may have felt that Roy's mess was as much as she could manage.

Roy slammed his bedroom door and fell on the bed. He was worn out. His elbow and knee had begun to sting. His brain was racing. Eric, politely, wiped his feet on the bedside rug and leapt up to join his friend. He was worn out, too. At the same time he was much relieved to be off the street. He remembered a dream he occasionally had of going to school in only his vest. This could've been worse!

Eric sat up and looked around. Roy's room was extremely full. It was full of clothes and comics, skates and model aeroplanes and fishing rods. Football posters covered the walls and a Hornby train set covered the floor. There were various abandoned collections of one thing or another; dead hobbies – a weaving kit, for instance, and a half-finished entry for a 'Blue Peter' painting competition. Because Roy rarely threw anything away, there was even (if you looked hard enough) a one-armed teddy

and a couple of baby books.

Roy stretched out and put his hands behind his head. 'Now what?' he said; and then, 'Hey, what about Hopper!' He threw his jockey cap in the air and caught it. 'Bet you're glad you're not a poodle, hey – or a chihuahua!'

Eric lay on the bed, his head on his paws and stared noncommittally at Roy. He was thinking about Joan Spooner. Roy had nearly given the game away there.

Roy said, 'Listen, what if –'

At that moment there were noises downstairs: a door closing; footsteps in the hall. Then a voice called out, 'Roy – you up there?'

Roy leapt from the bed, made a grab for his bag, opened the door, shouted 'Coming, Mum!', shut the door, took his grass-stained T-shirt off, put a clean one on – and left the room.

Then, almost immediately, he popped his head round the door. 'I'll be back in a bit,' and left again. And returned again: 'Whatever you do – don't bark!' And was gone.

Eric – once he had recovered from Roy's comings and goings – sat staring at the bedroom door and considered his situation. He was hungry, thirsty, dusty, *and*, of course, a dog. He was worried about his mum, who by this time would have his tea on and be worried about him. He was worried about Roy's mum. What if *she* came in?

Roy, meanwhile, having laid the table at a phenomenal speed (even for him) was now eating his tea, and – whenever his mum's back was turned – stealing Eric's. The tea was cold chicken, salad, tomatoes and potato crisps. There was plenty of bread and butter, and – warming in the oven – an apple pie which Mrs Turner had sent. Roy's mum was in and out doing various jobs: emptying his bag; fetching frozen peas from the freezer.

'Have some bread and butter,' she said as she passed his chair. And later, 'Use your fork!'

Roy bolted his food and wrapped Eric's scraps in paper hankies and crammed them into his pockets. When his mum went out to empty the pedal-bin, he left the table and raced upstairs. Eric was on the floor beside the train set. With no great enthusiasm, he was pushing a carriage along with his paw.

'Got you some tea,' said Roy. He emptied his pockets and arranged the hankies with their con-

tents on the bedside rug. There was a piece of squashed chicken, some crumbled crisps, a flat tomato and a ball of bread and butter.

'Eat up!' said Roy. 'I'll be back,' and he left.

Eric sniffed the food, discovered the full extent of his hunger, and ate the lot. After that he continued his exploration of Roy's room. He found a headless Action Man under the bed, and encountered a dreadful pong from one of Roy's socks. He found a comic on the floor which he began to read. Then Roy returned, this time with apple pie.

Eric ate the pie and Roy watched. It was exciting, smuggling food for a friend; but more than that – Roy discovered – it was surprisingly satisfying just to see him eat it.

Roy said, 'Hey, Eric, you could've pinched that ball!' He was remembering the cricket match. 'Run off with it, or fetched it from the pond' – where it usually ended up. 'You could've –'

'Roy!'

'Coming!' said Roy. He pulled a face, gave Eric a pat, and left.

Eric finished the pie and brushed the crumbs from his mouth. He resisted the urge to chew one of Roy's slippers. He snuffled once more under the bed. 'I wonder if he'll bring me a drink,' he thought. He practised miming thirst with an exaggerated panting. He trod on a marble.

Then, suddenly, in the gloomiest corner of the room where the bed met the wall, Eric felt a wobbly sensation in his legs, and had a strong conviction something was about to happen: something did. Seconds later, he experienced the now familiar tingling – like a mild electric shock, or pins and needles – in his paws; and an itch around his neck; and – this was new, or perhaps he hadn't noticed it before – a buzzing in his ears. He shut his eyes. His body wavered in the air like heat haze. In no time at all Eric the dog had dissolved and disappeared; Eric the boy had emerged to take his place.

Eric's first response to the change was to bang his head against the underside of the bed. He remembered the shrinking feeling he'd had at the baths. Of course, that was it; he *did* shrink when he turned into a dog ('So where does the rest of me go?') and enlarged when he turned back. And if he was under a bed at the time, he got stuck there; well, almost.

Eric flattened himself to the floor and with difficulty wriggled his way out. He looked around for his bag. When he opened it, he was dismayed to find his T-shirt tangled up with his wet trunks, his towel with dirt on it from his plimsolls, and only one sock. Eric – with a mixture of concern ('What's Mum going to say?') and relief ('I'm a boy!') – began to get dressed.

Meanwhile, down in the kitchen, Roy's problems were increasing. At first his mum had been too busy getting the tea on for herself and his dad to notice him. Gradually, however, her suspicions had become aroused. But it wasn't Roy's *actions* that did it: the amount he ate, the speed he ate at, and the fact that he seemed constantly on the move – all this was usual. What wasn't usual was his conversation. In an effort to camouflage his own excitement and avoid his mum's attentions, Roy had overdone it. 'Had a nice day, Mum?', 'Lovely tea!', and 'How's Mrs Turner?' (especially, 'How's Mrs Turner?') were simply not remarks Mrs Ackerman was accustomed to hear.

Finally, she set aside her mixing bowl and studied Roy. (He was loitering near the biscuit tin.) The first things she noticed were his grazes: elbow and knee. Then, as she applied the TCP, she noticed something else. 'Roy, where's your T-shirt?'

'I've got it on,' said Roy.

'I mean the one you went out in.'

'Er ... well,' said Roy.

'Stop mumbling!'

'It's in my room.' Roy shuffled uneasily. 'I, er ... had this accident.'

'What accident?' said his mum; and then, 'Go and fetch it!'

As Roy left the room, Mrs Ackerman put the seal on her disapproval. 'And take that cap off!' she said.

From now on things moved rapidly. Roy arrived in his room and discovered Eric. He was sitting on the bed reading a comic. Roy was openly amazed and secretly disappointed. Eric was shivering a little in his wet T-shirt and worrying about his lost sock. A conversation began. The subjects included the sock, the transformation, Hopper, Joan Spooner, and – finally – how to sneak Eric *out* of the house. Then –

bang! – the bedroom door flew open and Roy's mum discovered Eric.

Eric leapt to his feet. 'Good afternoon, Mrs Ackerman!'

And Roy said, 'Here's Eric!'

Mrs Ackerman merely frowned.

'I, er ... had this accident,' said Eric. He indicated his wet T-shirt.

'Did you?' said Mrs Ackerman.

'Roy said I could ... I could wait here till it dried.'

'Did he?' said Mrs Ackerman.

'I didn't want to bother you, Mum,' said Roy.

Then Eric grabbed his bag and said, 'Well, I'd better be going – thanks Roy!'

And on the stairs, Roy said, 'Don't mention it.'

And at the back door: 'See you tomorrow!'

After that Eric scuttled up the road and Roy took his time closing the door. He made rapid efforts to anticipate his mother's line of questioning. She was waiting for him, arms folded, in the kitchen.

'What's Eric been up to?' she said. 'His hands were filthy!'

And Roy said 'Er ... well.'

12

Farmer Wants Wife

Eric was almost home, when, at the corner of Clay Street and Apollo Road, he met Joan Spooner again. She was still on her bike, still on the pavement, and posting a letter in a letter-box.

'Hello, Eric!'

'Hello,' said Eric. 'Can't stop!' And he didn't.

Joan called after him, 'Where's Roy?'

'Who wants to know?' said Eric. 'He's your boy-friend, I bet!'

'No, he isn't.'

'You love him!' Eric was hurrying backwards up the road.

'He's got a dog!' shouted Joan. 'Says it's yours!'

'A what?'

'A dog!'

As the gap between them increased, so did the noise.

'Who has?'

'He has!'

'Y'what?'

'You heard!'

A woman with a baby scowled somewhat as she got caught in the middle. So did the baby. Then Eric reached his front gate and fell silent. Emily was in the garden riding her tricycle. His gran was there,

cutting a few roses. Most importantly, however, his mum was standing in the doorway with a cup of tea in her hand and a questioning look on her face.

'Hello, Eric!' said his gran. And Emily rang her bell for him. And his mum said, 'You're late. Where's your socks?'

'Hello, Gran!' said Eric. 'In my bag, well, er . . .' he lowered his voice, 'one of 'em.'

Emily left her tricycle and began tugging at her gran's dress. 'Want to whisper.'

She whispered, after which her gran said, 'She wants to do her S.O.N.G. for Eric.'

Mrs Banks continued to observe her son. He looked ill-at-ease. 'Is that T-shirt wet?'

'A little bit – what song?' He grabbed Emily and swung her round. 'A song for me, lovely!' Whereupon Emily (having immediately forgiven him for guessing it *was* a song) sang her song, although in fact her gran sang much of it. It was 'The Farmer Wants a Wife' or, in Emily's version, 'Farmer Wants Wife'. She had learnt it that morning at playschool and practised it in the afternoon at her gran's. Eric, meanwhile, sat on the step and demonstrated a keen interest in his sister, while hoping his mum might take a less than keen interest in him. She didn't.

'Eric, Roy hasn't got a dog, has he?'

Eric didn't hesitate. 'A dog? – no!'

'Only I think I saw him in the High Street with one.'

'Oh, *that* dog!' Eric did his best not to appear furtive. 'That wasn't Roy's. It sort of ... followed us.'

'Us? I didn't see you.'

'Ah!' said Eric.

Then his gran said 'Sh! This is the best bit.' And Emily, tunelessly but with much feeling, sang:

> 'Nurse wants dog,
> Nurse wants dog,
> E ... I ... E ... I
> Nurse wants dog.'

And his gran said, '*She* wants one.'

'I know,' said Eric.

'I've told your mum. She had a dog when she was two.'

Mrs Banks sipped her tea. 'That dog with Roy looked a bit like the one that got in the house,' she said.

Just then Mr Banks, in his postman's uniform, appeared at the gate. Emily was all for starting her performance again for his benefit. 'Want to whisper,' she said.

But Mrs Banks had other ideas. 'Come on, Charles – we'll be late.'

And he said, 'Right!' and went inside.

At this point Eric remembered his parents were going out and his gran was babysitting. He stood up and gave Emily a round of applause. She strutted a little and ran into the back garden.

His mum said, 'Let's see those hands!'

Reluctantly, Eric held them out. They didn't seem too bad to him. He'd spat on them and rubbed them on his jeans all the way from Roy's.

His gran also had a look. 'Like toads' backs!' she said.

Luckily, after that, what with the tea, and the getting ready to go out, and his gran being there, Eric avoided most of the trouble he might otherwise have expected. When his mum and dad left, he read a book and watched TV with his gran; it was raining outside. Emily made beds. She had a bag of cloth scraps and made beds for her dolls and teddies all over the room. She made beds for bits of Lego and lumps of Plasticine too, come to that.

After a while Eric lowered his book and stared unseeingly at the TV screen. He was thinking about the business of being a dog: how long would it go on? And shrinking: perhaps he should weigh himself next time, if there *was* a next time. He was thinking –

'Penny for them,' said his gran. And then, 'Cup of tea?'

'No, thanks,' said Eric. He watched his gran go out into the kitchen. He listened to the kettle being filled and the gas popping on. He looked down at Emily. She was making a bed in one of her

dad's slippers and singing quietly to herself.
  'Dickory, dickory,' Emily glanced up, caught Eric looking at her, and smiled, '...dog!'

13

Conversations

When Eric and Roy met on the paper-round next morning – it was Saturday – they had much to talk about.

In Freeth Street Roy said, 'What I want to know is, what was it like?'

'Being a dog?'

'No: changing.'

Eric thought for a moment. 'Scary!' he said.

Roy pushed a paper through a letter-box and felt an impatient hand pulling it from the other side. 'What could you see?' he said.

'Nothing. I had my eyes shut.'

In Fisher Road Roy said, 'I've been thinking – you must have shrunk, y'know.'

'I thought of that,' said Eric.

'So, where does the rest of you go?'

'That's what I wondered.' Eric leapt a low wall to deliver a paper.

Roy said, 'We could've weighed you; took your pawprints!' And he said, 'Listen – next time, if we cut a bit of your fur off, we could –'

'No,' said Eric.

'Only a bit!'

'No!'

In Stone Street they met up with the mastiff

again, barking as usual and rattling its chain.

'Can you tell what he's saying?' said Roy.

'He's saying, shove off!' said Eric.

'No, I mean, can you understand other dogs when you're one?'

And Eric, reluctant to confess that he couldn't, said, 'Sort of.'

Later, still in Stone Street, the subject turned to mums: 'My mum found crumbs where you'd been eating,' said Roy, and after that to Emily, and Emily's gran's idea that if she wanted a dog she should have one. 'That'd be good,' said Roy. And he thought, 'Two dogs – great!' And he said, 'If she *did* have one, it'd be your brother, y'know – think of that.'

In Vicarage Road they talked about Hopper and were glad it wasn't a school day, and codes, and not asking questions with either/or in them. Eric complained (as he had done before in Roy's room) about Roy giving the game away to Joan Spooner. Roy drew Eric's attention to the heavy responsibility (and heavy bags) he had been saddled with.

In Seymour Avenue Eric said, 'The German for dog is "hund",' which didn't interest Roy much; and, '"Dog" backwards spells "God",' which did.

Roy, in fact, was much struck by this notion. 'Hey, yes!' He kicked a cigarette packet into the gutter. 'Perhaps that's it – like reincantation, y'mean.'

'Carnation,' said Eric.

'Or a miracle!' said Roy.

When the round was finished, Eric went back to the shop to collect his wages. When he came out, Roy said, 'One year in a dog's life's supposed to be seven in a human's, isn't it?'

'Yes,' said Eric. He handed Roy his share of the money.

'Thanks,' said Roy. 'So y'see, what I've worked out is, if you were a ten-year-old dog, you'd really be seventy.'

'That doesn't sound right.'

'Yes it does,' said Roy. 'No wonder you wouldn't run about.'

On the way home, Roy tentatively raised one last question. It had been in his mind – off and on – ever since Eric had turned back into a boy. 'Listen, Eric,' he fiddled with his cap, 'I've been thinking,' and tried to keep the hopeful tone out of his voice, 'when might you change again?'

'Dunno,' said Eric.

'Only I was wondering, perhaps if you thought hard about it, you might sort of … *make* it happen.'

At that moment a man stepped out onto the pavement farther up the road and shouted, 'Roy!' It was his dad.

Roy looked at his watch and began to run. 'I've got to go!'

'Right,' said Eric.

'Listen, don't forget, if you *do* change –'

'I know,' said Eric: 'come round.'

Roy ran backwards up the road. 'And don't forget, if you *do* come round –'

'I know,' said Eric, and cupped his hands to his mouth: 'Howl!'

14

Mongrel

Eric and Roy didn't see each other again until Monday morning, although Roy did try to get to Eric's on Sunday morning, but was prevented by his mum. On Saturday Roy was away all day at his grandparents' house. Sunday, it rained.

On Monday, on the way to school, Roy showed Eric some foreign coins his grandad had given him. When Kenny Biggs joined them, he showed him, too. Kenny, however, was interested in other things. 'What happened to that dog?'

At this point Roy couldn't resist the urge to be mysterious. After all, where was the fun in having a secret, if nobody knew you had it? 'Hard to say,' he said. And later, 'That'd be telling!' And later still, 'Sorry, Kenny – it's a secret.'

Eric, of course, didn't approve of Roy's behaviour, but apart from the odd nudge there was little he could do.

Then, as they neared the school gates, the subject turned inevitably to Hopper. 'I don't think he really missed you,' said Kenny; 'too busy batting.'

And Roy said, 'Y'know, when you think about it, we've got the fourth years on us, and the second years have got us on them, and the first years have got the second years on them.'

'And the infants have got the first years,' said Eric. 'And the playschool kids have got the infants!'

'And the babies have got everybody!' Kenny said.

During assembly Mr Blocker sang a hymn, read a prayer, and complained about litter. He also presented a number of swimming badges and made an announcement about Sports Day, due to take place on the coming Saturday.

There was a buzz of excitement when Sports Day was mentioned. Under cover of it – or so he thought – Roy said, 'Let's go to the library at playtime, and look at dog books.'

'That's what I was going to say,' said Eric.

And Mrs Jessop said, 'Roy!'

For the first part of the morning Class Three had a maths lesson with Mr Cork. He had drawn a large graph on the marker-board. It was based on a survey of children's names in the school, which some of the girls had done. According to this survey there were eleven Traceys and eight Garys. At the other extreme there was one Shane, one Angelita and one Eric.

Eric pretended to be pleased to be the only Eric, but privately rather envied the more numerous Michaels and Jonathans.

Roy (there were two Roys) said, 'If they'd called you Robin, you'd have been Robin Banks – think of that!'

At playtime Eric and Roy avoided the teacher on duty and sneaked into the library. From their previous work on dogs, they knew exactly where to look. Roy was interested in reading about Norfolk terriers. He especially wanted to see a picture of one. Eric's interest was more general. Now that he absolutely knew he'd turned into a dog – and not once, but twice – he increasingly wanted to find out why. The urge was scientific. He didn't know yet how to proceed, but dog books seemed as good a starting point as any.

Unfortunately, each boy had barely laid hands on the book of his choice when Mr Blocker, with a cup of tea in one hand and a starting pistol in the other, entered the library.

'You boys!' he said.

'Sir!' said Eric.

'What are you up to?'

'Studying, Sir,' said Eric.

'Dog books,' said Roy, and held his up as proof.

Mr Blocker, however, was an experienced head.

He prided himself he knew what studying was, and what fooling around was, too. He waved his pistol at them and told them to leave.

At dinner time Eric and Roy found places on Joan and Alison's table. Alison wanted to hear more about Roy's dog – or was it Eric's? – that Joan had told her about. Roy dropped a couple of hints and Eric gave him a kick under the table.

Alison said, 'I heard of a dog once that put a bone in your bed, if it liked you.'

'I heard of one that howled if you stroked the cat,' said Joan.

After dinner Eric and Roy avoided the dinner ladies and sneaked into the infant library. Eric found a Ladybird book on dogs. Roy got waylaid a little with a book called *Where's Spot?*. It was about a puppy. You had to lift the flap on each page to find where it was hiding. Roy thoroughly enjoyed it.

Suddenly, a man's face with a cigarette in it appeared at the window. It was Mr Moody, the caretaker. He knocked on the window and gestured for them to leave. He mouthed a single word through the glass: 'Out!'

In the afternoon Class Three had a drama lesson with Mr Cork. Joan and Alison asked Eric and Roy to be in their play.

'Joan wants you to be in our play,' said Alison.

'No, *she* wants you to,' said Joan.

'What's it about?' said Eric.

'It's called "The Mad Professor's Daughter",' said Joan. 'It's about this girl who comes to a school, and she's dressed all in black, and she asks the other girls to go home with her.'

'Any eating in it?' said Roy. He'd been in a play

once, about a picnic. There had been real sandwiches and real pop.

'No,' said Joan. 'Anyway, these girls go with this girl, you see, and her father – he's the mad professor – he drugs them and chains them up in his dungeon.'

'Where'd you get the idea from?' said Roy.

'Alison made it up,' said Joan.

'No, *you* did,' said Alison.

'Who's going to be the daughter?' said Eric.

'Me!' said Alison and Joan.

At the end of the day Eric and Roy made one more effort to further their education and look at library books. This time, for a while, they were successful. Roy, in fact, soon found what he was looking for: a picture of a Norfolk terrier. 'Hey, Eric – look at this!' But Eric was intent on his own book and did not reply.

Roy said, 'This dog's different from you, y'know. Your ears were flappier, and you had more fur. You're not a Norfolk terrier.' He considered the matter for a moment. 'Sorry, Eric – you're a mongrel!'

Just then Mrs Jessop entered the library. She had her coat on and was carrying a handbag and a briefcase.

Eric leapt to his feet and improvised an alibi. 'We're doing a dog project, Miss!'

'An advanced dog project,' said Roy.

But Mrs Jessop was not impressed. She had a quick look round the library to see what they were *really* up to, and told them to go home.

Out in the street Roy said, 'Y'know, this *is* a dog project, when you think about it.' And he said, 'We could find out more about dogs than

97

even the books know. You could interview 'em!'

Eric said, 'Don't you call me a mongrel!'

On the way home Eric and Roy arranged to go to the Tat Bank Library after tea. There'd be dog books there all right, and no interference.

When he arrived home and entered the kitchen, Eric found his mum sitting at the table reading a paper.

'Seen my library ticket, Mum?' he said.

'Sitting-room sideboard,' said Mrs Banks, without looking up, 'top drawer, right.'

Eric left the room and returned shortly after. Mrs Banks continued to read. 'What are you going to the library for?'

'Dog books,' said Eric, and immediately regretted his words.

'Dog books?' Mrs Banks lowered her paper and looked closely at Eric. He had the feeling she was trying to read *him*. She said, 'Is Roy going?'

'Yes,' said Eric.

'In this weather – to a library?'

'Yes. It's a sort of ... project.'

Mrs Banks continued to scrutinize her son. 'Hmm!' she said.

When they reached the library, Eric and Roy headed straight for the dog books in the children's section.

'Here's a good 'un,' said Roy, almost before he'd taken it from the shelf: '*Wild Dogs and Working Dogs.*'

'I'm having this,' said Eric: '*A Closer Look at Dogs.*'

Roy said, 'This one's got careers for dogs in it. Hey, we could find you a job!'

'It says here,' said Eric, '"A St Bernard is a hundred times heavier than a chihuahua".'

'I could've told you that,' said Roy. Then he said, 'You could be a guide dog – a guard dog!'

'"The Greeks believed there was a dog with three heads",' said Eric.

'A gun dog!' said Roy.

Half an hour later Eric and Roy emerged from the library and stood squinting in the bright sunlight. Each was carrying three books, the maximum allowed. Eric had one of his open. 'It says here,' he said.

'Hello, Miss!' shouted Roy.

Eric looked up, just in time to see Mrs Jessop go riding by on her bicycle.

'Hello boys!' Mrs Jessop, for her part, had time to notice the armfuls of books Eric and Roy were carrying, and the library they were leaving. As she turned the corner, she felt a twinge of guilt. They really *were* doing a project!

Eric and Roy watched her go. Then Eric said, 'It says here: "The dog is essentially an animal of the chase: enduring, patient, intelligent and fleet of foot".' He smiled and stuck out his chest. 'That's me!'

15

The Dog File

For the remainder of that week Eric and Roy
continued to give much thought to the question:
When would Eric change again? (or, as the days
passed: *Would* he change again?). Eric himself had
trouble getting to sleep at night, and woke up each
morning in a state of some anxiety. Roy couldn't
sleep either; he kept thinking (hoping) he could hear
a howling dog. During the day he stayed as close to
Eric as he could for as long as he could. He made
frequent – too frequent, Eric said – enquiries about
how he was feeling.

The other question which occupied them was, of
course, *why* was he changing? This, in fact, took
more of their time than the first question. They
talked incessantly about it, read dog books to each
other, and made notes, even – well, Eric made notes.
Inevitably, their school work suffered. Roy,
especially, heard very little that his teachers had to
say during this period.

On Tuesday morning Eric came to school with one
dog book and a pocket-sized clip file, complete with
paper and cardboard section-dividers. It also had
a pencil down the spine. It was a so-far-unused
Christmas present from his gran. Roy came to school

– staggered would be nearer the truth – with all three of his books, plus his dad's *Guinness Book of Records* and a bag of apple peel and carrot tops for the rabbit.

As they neared the school gates, Eric showed Roy the file and explained its purpose. 'We're going to collect data,' he said. It was a phrase he had come upon inside the lid of his junior science kit.

'What's data?'

'Notes,' said Eric, 'lists and things, from the dog books.'

'How about tracings?'

'The question is, what makes a boy turn into a dog? We might not need tracings for that.'

'But I *like* tracings,' said Roy.

In the playground, Roy brought up the subject of colour-blindness. Dogs were supposed to be colour-blind, that's what he'd read.

'I wasn't colour-blind,' said Eric.

'You should've been,' Roy said; 'according to this.'

He also found the rarest breed of dog in his *Guinness Book of Records*. 'You should've been a Chinese Fighting Dog, they're worth quids!' And he said, 'They eat dogs in China, y'know.'

Later that morning there was a lull in the classroom. Mr Cork, with the help of a few girls, was pinning children's work up on the walls, though he was due to leave on Friday and would take most of it with him. Mrs Jessop was in the staffroom with the slow readers. Eric opened his dog book and began to read; Roy did likewise.

After a time, Eric said, 'I might not be the first – think of that!'

'The first what?' said Roy. As an aid to concen-

102

tration, he had his hands over his ears, though he heard Eric well enough.

'Boy to turn into a dog,' said Eric. 'Listen to this: "The screen's most versatile acting dog was Teddy" –'

'That's no name for a dog,' said Roy.

'"In one remarkable routine, filmed entirely without a break, Teddy opened a kitchen door, lit the stove with a match held between his teeth, filled a kettle at the sink, put it on the stove, and then, picking up a broom, swept the floor. He could play comedy or drama with equal ease, never missed a cue, and his pheno ... pheno ..."' ('Phemonimal!' said Roy) *"phenomenal* memory put many a two-legged co-star to shame."'

Eric and Roy were silent for a moment.

Roy said, 'No dog could do all that!'

'That's what I think.' Eric opened his bag and took out the clip file. 'I bet he was a boy.'

Eric and Roy were much taken with the idea that other boys before Eric could have turned into dogs. Even on the way home from school, they were still discussing it. As they window-shopped in Russell's sweet shop, Eric spoke of the 'wolf boys' in India he'd read about. Perhaps there was a clue there. Roy said he was sure there was an 'elephant man', but couldn't remember where he'd heard of him. 'Anyway, he never turned into an elephant, I don't think. He only looked like one.'

Then Kenny Biggs joined them, picked up a snatch of their conversation, and offered a thought of his own. 'I heard a talking dog once.'

'When?' said Eric.

'Where?' said Roy.

'On the radio, months ago. It was Australian.'

'Hey, I remember that!' said Roy.

'Yes,' said Kenny. 'It could say "mum" and "sausage and egg".' And he said (Kenny was clearly intent on being useful), 'I heard a singing cat as well.'

On Wednesday Eric and Roy continued to speculate. At nine o'clock, as they lined up in the playground, Roy said, 'I've been thinking – you could've dreamt it, y'know.'

'No,' said Eric. 'Anyway, if I dreamt it, what were you doing?'

'Perhaps I dreamt it as well.'

'And Hopper?'

'Yes.'

'And Kenny – and my mum – and yours?'

'It's possible,' said Roy. Then, as a glare from Mrs Jessop cut short the conversation, 'Anything is!'

Later, in the classroom, during an art lesson with Mr Cork, Roy took up the idea again. He was still not convinced. 'We could've dreamt all of it,' he said;

'Hopper and everything. We could be dreaming now.'

'Pinch yourself, then,' said Eric. 'Better still, I'll pinch you. No, even better, I'll stick these compasses in you. If you yell out, you were dreaming.'

'That won't prove it,' said Roy. He smiled and edged away. 'I could be dreaming I'm yelling.'

That afternoon at two o'clock all the third and fourth years trooped out of the school, up Rolph Street, down Ethel Street, across Joining's Bank and into Hobbes's recreation ground. This was where the school sports would be held on Saturday. Today, however, it was the heats, plus demonstrations of technique from various members of staff: Mr Hodge and Mr Cork (baton changing), Mrs Jessop (rounders ball) and Mr Blocker (starting pistol).

The weather was warm and sunny. When they were not competing, Eric and Roy sat on the grass with the rest of Class Three and watched the others, and talked.

'It says here,' said Roy (he still had one of his books with him), '"Each year more than four thousand British postmen are bitten by dogs".'

'My dad never gets bitten,' said Eric.

' ",The Post Office procedure, following an assault, is to send a letter of complaint to the owner" – hey, this is good! – "which the postman has to deliver"!'

Just then Joan Spooner and Caroline Wicks came hobbling towards them. They were tied together with a skipping rope, practising for the three-legged race.

Joan said, 'What're you reading – a dog book, I'll bet!' And she said, 'They're mad about dogs, them two.'

'Where's Alison?' said Eric, but got no reply, as the girls at that point tumbled over and rolled noisily away. In any case he knew where she was: she was tied to Sheila Smith. Joan and Alison had quarrelled earlier in the day and were 'not speaking'.

Then Roy said, 'There's a dog!' The dog – a black-and-white collie – was sniffing along the perimeter fence a short way off. From time to time it paused and peed against one of the wooden posts.

'It's marking its territory,' said Eric. 'I read about that.'

'Territory?' Roy laughed. 'It doesn't own all this – it's Hobbes's!' He turned and threw a handful of grass at Tony Abell, who had previously thrown one at him. He said, 'Hey, Eric – I've been thinking – did you ever . . . ?' He nodded towards the now departing dog. 'Y'know . . .'

'No!' said Eric.

'Not even . . . ?'

'No!'

At that moment there was a commotion down on the track. Mr Blocker could be seen looking particularly fierce. Mr Hodge was running towards the main gate. Hopper, it seemed, had just thrown the rounders ball into the road.

'It's a record!' said Roy.

On Thursday, Rolfe Street Primary was closed for polling. There was a bye-election. Eric went to town with his mum in the morning to get a pair of walking boots. In the afternoon Roy came round. The two of them spent their time in the garden. They paddled in Emily's playpool (she was at her gran's) and sat in her Wendy house. Eric showed Roy some work he'd done in the clip file (now known as the 'Dog File'). 'It's a list of theories; it's not finished yet.'

Roy took the file and began to read:

'1.   THE NOT-THE-FIRST THEORY. (You should've put that second, then.)
2.   THE RAYS-FROM-SPACE THEORY.
3.   THE REINCARNATION THEORY.
4.   THE –'

'That's as far as I've got,' said Eric.

Roy stuck his head out of the side of the Wendy house – it was made of plastic sheeting – and looked up at the sky. 'What about "The Chinese-Fighting-Dog Theory"?'

'That's not a theory,' said Eric.

'What about ...' Roy turned and made a grab for Eric's ankle, '"*The Body-Snatcher's Theory*"!'

'Let go – what's that?' said Eric.

'Dunno,' said Roy; 'but it sounds good.'

Roy, in fact, was remembering a film that had been shown on TV a couple of months ago: 'The

Invasion of the Body-Snatchers'. He'd only seen the trailer, and not all of that; his mum had switched it off. Even so – from the title alone – it surely had *some* relevance to Eric's situation.

At three o'clock Roy accompanied Eric to collect Emily from her gran's. Eric's gran gave each of them an ice lolly from her freezer. Emily had been grumpy when they arrived, not wanting to leave. But, with a lolly in her hand, she soon cheered up. Eric and Roy

took it in turns to push her doll's pushchair, leaving Emily free to concentrate on licking.

Roy's lolly was the first to go, then Eric's. Emily's – though it dribbled a little down her arm and on her T-shirt – lasted longer.

Eric said, 'I'll give you 5p for a lick.'

'No!' said Emily.

'10p.'

'No!'

'£10!'

'No!'

Eric laughed. He often played this game with Emily, just for the fun of hearing her say 'no'. He loved, above all, the *certainty* with which she said it. Then Roy joined in. 'I'll give you all the houses in this street.'

'No!'

'In this town!' said Eric.

'In the world!' said Roy.

'No!'

'I'll give you Eric,' said Roy.

'I'll give you Roy!' said Eric.

Emily sucked the final lump of her lolly into her mouth, licked her sticky thumb and stared up at them. 'Lo!' she said.

On Friday morning when Eric woke up he was still a boy. When they met on the paper-round, Roy – automatically almost – said, 'Anything?'

Eric shook his head.

'How're you feeling now?'

'Normal.'

'It's been a whole week, y'know.'

'I know.' Eric could sense Roy's disappointment and was about to comment on it, when, suddenly, a small boy came up to him and asked where he could get a puppy from.

'How should I know?' said Eric.

The boy became immediately confused. 'Well, I heard ... a big girl told me ... on the dinner table ...' he fiddled with the buttons of his jumper '... you was the one to ask.'

'Joan, I'll bet!' said Roy.

'That big girl's up the creek,' said Eric.

'Oh!' said the boy.

And Roy said, 'Tell y'mum to try the R.S.P.C.A.'

An hour later, in his room, as he gathered his school things together, Eric considered the extent to which his secret was spreading. Only Roy knew everything, of course; but quite a few others (Hopper and Kenny, Joan and Alison, not to mention Caroline and Sheila) knew *something*, or thought they did. And now there was this infant...

Meanwhile, the main 'dropper-of-hints' himself was on his way to call for Eric. He had a bag on his shoulder, a ball at his feet and a book in his hand. He'd been reading about the relative merits of dog-baskets and kennels. Roy, in truth, had a small secret of his own. He was swotting up (mostly at home) everything he could find about the care of dogs: grooming, bedding, vitamins and health, dogs and the law – everything. But he'd so far said nothing to Eric about it, in case his motives were misunderstood.

The main events at school that day were a long speech about Sports Day from Mr Blocker in the morning, and the departure of Mr Cork in the afternoon. It was the end of his school practice. There were presents for him (and his rabbit), and cheers and tears, and requests for autographs, and increasingly nosy questions. What was his first name? Where did he live? Had he got a girlfriend? Could they write to him? Then he was gone, and the sudden silence and the bare walls (he'd taken most of their work with him) left everyone feeling rather solemn for a while.

On the way home, Eric and Roy discussed Mr

Cork's merits, and compared him with other students they had known.

'I'm going to be a student,' said Roy.

'What're you going to study?'

'Something,' Roy said. He balanced along the wall outside the Ebenezer Chapel, and fell off before the end. He threw his jockey cap in the air, aiming to graze the overhanging branch of a tree. And he said, 'Hey, *werewolves* – think of that!'

16

Sports Day

On Saturday Eric did his paper-round with Roy and came home as usual for his second breakfast. His mum was in the kitchen making a shopping list. Emily was eating a bowl of Coco Pops. She had the help of a small teddy and a plastic frog, who were grouped around the bowl.

She said, 'See my hat!'

Emily was wearing her Bo-Peep hat in readiness for a fancy-dress competition in the afternoon. (It was one of the extra events at the school sports.) She would've worn her Bo-Peep dress and been carrying her Bo-Peep crook, too, if her mother had let her.

'Very nice,' said Eric. 'I'll give you 5p for it.'

'No!' said Emily.

'Don't start all that,' said Mrs Banks. 'She's got a bus to catch.'

'I'll give it her anyway,' said Eric, who was feeling generous, having just been paid. After that he sat down at the table, overtook Emily in the eating of *his* bowl of Coco Pops, got up, and left the room.

Mrs Banks called after him, 'We're going to town!'

'Right!' said Eric, on the stairs.

'Your dad'll be back about twelve!'

'Right!' said Eric, from the landing.

'Your sports kit's in your bag!'

Eric entered his room and crossed to the dressing-table. He opened a drawer, felt beneath a pile of socks and took out the Oxo tin in which he kept his money. He tipped it onto the bed and added more from his pocket. He began to sort it into £1 piles. Eric had reached £5.45 when suddenly something happened which caused him to lose count: he turned into a dog.

Eric crouched on the bed and shut his eyes as the usual *unusual* sensations rushed upon him: the itching and the curious tingling, the shrinking feeling, the wet nose and the flappy ears. His body — if he could have seen it — had gone all blurry, like a bad photograph. His clothes had ceased to fit.

At that moment the phone rang.

'Eric – answer that, will you?'

'I would if I could,' thought Eric. He opened his eyes and looked around.

'Eric – the phone!'

'Sorry, Mum.' One of his trainers slipped off his shrunken foot and fell to the floor. The phone stopped ringing.

Eric pricked his ears. He could hear his mum talking in the hall, followed soon after by the 'ping' as the receiver was replaced.

Then, seconds later: 'Eric, we're off!'

Footsteps in the hall.

Emily's little piping voice, 'Bye-bye, Eric!'

'Eric?' His mum again, and sounding puzzled. 'You all right?'

Emily's little clumping feet on the stairs.

Rapidly Eric scrambled off the bed and hid under it.

Then, again, his mum: 'No, Emily – come on, we'll miss the bus. Bye, Eric!'

'Bye-bye!'

And the front door slammed.

Eric stayed where he was for a moment and endeavoured to recover his wits. Eventually, he spotted a golf ball under the bed, which he thought he'd lost. He picked it up in his mouth and carried it onto the rug. His movements were, of course, hampered by his clothes. As he wriggled free of his shorts and T-shirt, the thought in his mind was: 'If this lasts all day, I'll miss the long jump.' His underpants were the trickiest to get out of; his socks, the easiest; he just tugged them off with his teeth.

Eric sat on his haunches and studied the golf ball. 'Now what?' he thought. Well, at least he felt less panic this time; nor were there any swimming attendants to worry about. He wandered onto the landing. The smell of Emily's bubble bath – she'd tipped too much in as usual – filled the air.

Eric considered his options. He could try to get out of the house – through a window, say – and go to Roy's. He could stay where he was till his dad arrived, and hope to change back before he was found. He could ... what else could he do? Eric decided there was nothing else he could do. He also decided that climbing out of windows would be ill-advised. Besides, assuming he *would* change back, he preferred to do it in the privacy of his own home. Meanwhile – he stepped into his parents' room – perhaps he would just ... nosy around for a while.

And 'nosy' was the word: for a boy who was a dog, the house was an absolute map of smells. In his parents' room alone there was Lily of the Valley talc and Old Spice aftershave, Johnson's Wax on the chest of drawers and Windolene on the windows, a hard-to-describe 'overcoat' smell near the wardrobe and a faint hint of soot in the fireplace. Even his mum's book on a chair by the bed had its own smell; even her clock!

After a time Eric left the room and continued to prowl somewhat aimlessly about. He looked in at Emily's room. She had a large Snoopy dog sitting in one corner. Eric resisted the urge to have a fight with it, and went downstairs. In the hall he was startled by a free newspaper which came suddenly hurtling through the letter-box and almost hit him on the head. He glanced briefly at the front page and went into the sitting-room. He walked in and out of the furniture. He looked out of the window. He jumped up and sat in an easy chair. He became motionless.

At this point, Eric – could he have done so – would probably have drummed with his fingers on the arm of the chair. The truth is, he was becoming bored. It appeared there was not a lot you could actually *do* as a dog on your own, and locked up. 'That's why they like going for walks,' he thought. And then he noticed the television.

Eric left the chair and trotted over to it. Luckily, it was switched on at the wall. He put his nose against the on/off button (it had a smell too!) and pressed. The screen glowed and a voice informed him that what he really needed was a BMX bike. He tried changing the channel, but was unable to operate the control, which was a dial. He went back to his chair, turned round in a complete circle, and settled down with his chin on his paws to watch the programme, whatever it was.

As Eric watched the usual Saturday morning mixture of pop songs and cartoons, his thoughts wandered. During a Yogi Bear cartoon, he found

himself remembering the Australian talking dog. He sat up in his chair and tried saying 'sausage and egg' once or twice, but without success. He also kept an eye on the time (there was a clock in the room). He meant to be back upstairs and under his bed (or in his wardrobe, even) long before his dad came home.

At about twenty to twelve, in the middle of a soft drink ad., Eric began to feel thirsty. He went into the kitchen, leapt on a chair and from there made it to the draining-board. He inspected the water in which the breakfast washing-up was standing, and decided to catch drips from the tap instead. He put out his tongue.

At that moment something else happened. The back door opened, Eric's dad came in, and – seconds later – Eric himself went out. Eric got the impression his dad was in a hurry. He was snatched so fast from the draining-board, for instance, he still had his tongue out. And hustled down the garden path and dumped on the pavement before he could even bark. His dad, moreover, spoke only three words the whole time: 'You again!' and 'Out!' Later, however, Eric did hear a fourth, which was 'Eric'. This came in a variety of intonations and volumes: 'Eric? ERIC? *ERIC!*', from different parts of the house and garden. His dad was looking for him, it seemed. Eric sat on the pavement in some confusion and dismay. He considered his 'crimes' as his dad would see them: the unattended house, the unlocked door, the interloping dog, and the TV ('Oh, no – I left it on!'). He considered his dad's crime, too: coming home early!

Across the road, and unobserved by Eric, a small

cat sat hidden in a hedge observing him. It was the one he'd chased two weeks before. Two weeks older, two weeks wiser, the cat bristled a little, but remained hidden. Eric, meanwhile, had reached a decision. He couldn't stay where he was and he couldn't get back in. There was only one place he could go. He set off purposefully up the road.

When Eric reached Roy's house, he hung around for a while hoping to see Roy or be seen by him. But no face appeared at any of the windows and no one came out. He trotted up the drive and sat on the front lawn. There was a faint smell of petrol in the air, and cut grass. He waited: still no one came, no one saw him. At last – though feeling distinctly silly about it – Eric did what he had to. He braced his legs, threw back his head, and howled.

When Roy heard Eric (he never doubted it *was* Eric), he was in his room. He was sorting a few toys for his little cousins to play with downstairs. They were there on a visit with his Uncle Colin and Auntie Val.

Roy rushed to the window and, sure enough, there was Eric (looking worried) on the lawn. He opened the window and stuck his head out. 'Eric?'

'Woof!' said Eric.

'Wait there – I'll be down!'

Rapidly Roy gathered up whatever toys and games he could lay his hands on. He raced downstairs, almost threw them into the sitting-room, said: 'Back in a minute!' (luckily his mum was in the kitchen), and shot outside. Eric was glad to see him. He'd come to the conclusion that it was lonely being a dog. And Roy, though his motives were different,

was glad to see Eric, especially *this* Eric. The two friends smiled, and one of them wagged his tail.

Roy's head was full of questions, which he knew would have to wait. Apart from anything else, he had to get back before he was missed.

'Listen, Eric – I can't come yet – we've got visitors!' He moved backwards towards the door. Eric followed him. 'No – not you – Mum'd have a fit!'

Eric looked mournful and felt the urge to whine.

Roy said, 'Here, wait in the garage.' He led the way.

A voice – Roy's mum – called from the house: 'Roy?'

'Lie low!' Roy said. 'I'll be back!' And he left.

Eric, feeling shut out and unwanted, snuffled around in the garage for a while. He found a pile of

119

newspapers in a corner behind a mower. He lay low.

Eric lay low, as it turned out, till almost one o'clock. Roy did his best to get away, but it wasn't easy. He had to entertain his cousins, show some interest in his uncle and aunt, and eat a light lunch. During lunch Roy suddenly 'remembered' he'd volunteered to help with the chairs for Sports Day. His mum had her doubts about this, and his dad said it was no excuse for eating like a python, but they let him go. A minute later he was in the street with his sports kit in his bag, money to spend, a couple of apples, and Eric.

Eric was confused. He was following Roy because he didn't want to be on his own. But he didn't want to be in the street either. On the other hand (or paw), what else could he do? Roy, meanwhile, had begun eating an apple. He bit off a piece and held it out. Eric, despite his troubles, ate it up.

Roy said, 'I'll have to go to the sports, y'know. I'm in the relay.' He swopped his bag to his other shoulder. 'We've had it for the three-legged, though, haven't we?'

'Woof!' agreed Eric. He hadn't thought of that.

'We'd win the five-legged, though,' Roy said. 'We'd walk it!'

At the corner of Clay Street and Apollo Road, Roy looked at his watch. It was ten past one. The sports were due to start at two o'clock. He said, 'Let's go to the park for a bit.'

'That's what I was thinking,' thought Eric.

'And after that we'll go to the sports. They've got a pavilion there, they've got a groundsman's hut.' (He was thinking of places where Eric might hide, if he had to.) 'After that we'll ... think of something.'

120

At the park gates, going in, Roy and Eric met Kenny Biggs coming out. He was kicking a ball and eating a stick of rock. Behind him – some way behind – came little Malky on a tricycle. He was eating a stick of rock, too.

Kenny said, 'Hello, Roy – hey, you've got that dog again!'

'Where'd you get y'rock?' said Roy.

'Russell's. Whose dog is he really?'

'Give us a bite and I'll tell you.' As he spoke, Roy lunged for the ball, and dribbled off with it onto the grass.

Meanwhile, Eric had *his* eye on a stick of rock. He was sitting up close to Malky's now stationary tricycle and staring hopefully at its rider. But Malky, no matter how little he was, knew what was going on. He laughed and bounced on his saddle and clutched his rock more tightly. 'Mine!' he shouted.

Then, impulsively – or perhaps he just wanted to see what would happen – he held it out. Eric, to his credit, hesitated. He felt suddenly guilty. Taking sweets from a small child when you were a dog was wrong, and for that matter unhygienic. At the same time it was a particularly large stick of rock, far too big for Malky ...

At that moment Alison Jukes came riding up on her bicycle, followed closely by Joan Spooner on hers. They were friends again, it seemed.

'Hello, Malky!' said Alison.

'It's that dog again!' said Joan.

'And he wants y'rock,' Alison said.

Whereupon Malky immediately snatched it away and took a bite himself. Eric, with mixed feelings, trotted over to join Kenny and Roy. Having failed to agree a swop, they were kicking the ball back and forth between them.

Joan said, 'Whose dog is he really?'

'He's not telling,' said Kenny. 'I don't think he knows.'

'I know,' said Roy. 'I know more than you think.' He turned his attention to Malky. 'I'll give you half this apple for a bite of rock.'

Malky studied the apple.

'Don't you, Malky,' said Alison. 'You keep it.'

'Ask him whose dog it is,' said Kenny.

Then Roy had an idea. 'Listen, Malky – if you give me a bite, this dog'll shake hands with you.' He crouched and whispered to Eric, 'Go on, Eric, be a sport!'

Eric considered the matter. He could see that Roy was getting carried away; also, by rights, if any rock *was* going, *he* should get it. Then again ... He looked across at Malky's little beaming face, and he thought, 'Why not?'

Eric approached Malky, who by this time had left his tricycle and joined the others on the grass.

'On the command "shake hands",' said Roy, 'this dog will ... shake hands.' Then he said, 'Shake ... hands!'

Eric at once held out his paw. For a moment Malky was overcome with shyness, but of course he was delighted, too. Soon he was holding Eric's paw in his own sticky hand and shaking it proudly.

'There!' said Roy. 'Now, on the command "bite rock", this boy will ...' Roy got his rock, though the amount was carefully monitored by Kenny. After that there was a general rush to see what else Eric could do.

'Get him to say "How do you do?",' said Joan.

'Like that Australian dog,' Kenny said.

'Get him to count!' said Alison.

Roy – flushed with success – got Eric to count. 'What's two plus two?' he said.

'Woof, woof, woof, woof!' barked Eric. (*He* was getting carried away.)

'Six take away four?' said Roy.

'Woof, woof!'

'The square root of nine?' (Roy was good at maths.)

'Woof, woof, woof!' (So was Eric.)

It was about now that Kenny and Alison exchanged puzzled looks. They realized something was going on (so did Joan), but couldn't quite tell what it was.

'It's a trick,' said Alison.

'No it's not; he's just a brainy dog,' said Roy.

Then Joan said, 'All right then – what's four hundred and ninety-six plus two hundred and eighty-three?'

Eric hardly hesitated. 'Woof, woof, woof, woof, woof, woof, woof –'

'Hang on, hang on,' said Roy. 'We'll be here for ever.'

'What's the capital of Peru?' said Kenny.

'What's the time?' said Joan.

Eric made no reply but continued to look expectantly at his audience. It was as though he was waiting for a question he *could* answer, which, in truth, he was. He hadn't had this much attention since his tenth birthday.

Roy said, 'Wait a minute; let me have a go.' And he said, 'Here's a good 'un: Which of these girls do y'like the best – her or her?'

Eric cocked his head on one side, then the other. He looked Joan and Alison up and down. The first thought in his mind was, 'Neither!' However, secretly (so secretly he hadn't even told Roy, though Roy knew anyway) Alison was his favourite. (And, of course, *she* knew as well.)

While Eric was seeming to make his mind up, Kenny said, 'How's he going to choose?'

'He can point,' said Joan.

'That's it,' Roy said; 'point!'

And so, eventually, Eric put out his paw and pointed at Alison. She laughed. 'He *is* a brainy dog!' she said. And then, 'Have a crisp!'

After this the gathering began to break up. Kenny had to take Malky home and get ready for the sports. Joan and Alison needed to collect their kit.

As she rode off, Alison tossed a final crisp to Eric. He, despite its wayward flight through the air, caught it and crunched it up.

As she rode off, Joan called out, 'Whose dog is he *really*? What's his name?'

Roy paused for a second and said, 'Eric.'

'What?'

'Eric.'

'I can't hear you!'

'It's just as well,' said Roy. He watched Joan disappear through the gates. 'You'd never believe it.'

17

Bo-Peep

When Eric and Roy arrived at Hobbes's recreation ground, they found the entrance decorated with coloured flags. A large banner announcing the sports flapped gently in the breeze. There was an ice-cream van parked in the street, with a queue of customers already formed. A baby in a pram nearby was bawling.

Rolfe Street Primary School Sports Day was, in fact, rather more than a Sports Day. For one thing the parent–teacher association took the opportunity to raise money for the school fund. There were various stalls: bottle, cake, white elephant, nearly-new. There were games such as skittles and penalty prize. There was a Punch and Judy show, a fancy-dress parade and a Boys' Brigade band.

The other thing which made Sports Day special was the attitude of Mr Blocker. Most heads have something in their school which they take a particular interest in. It could be the school play or the school choir; the school dinners, even. In Mr Blocker's case it was Sports Day. The story was that he had once run for the county, but no details were available.

Eric and Roy passed beneath the flapping banner and joined the growing crowd. It was two o'clock.

Already the stalls had begun selling, and the games and competitions were in progress. The athletic events wouldn't begin until two-thirty. Councillor Mrs Beanland would be there to start the first race and, later, present the cup to the winning house.

As he wandered between the stalls, Roy had a go on the hoop-la and inadvertently won a bottle of tomato ketchup. He tried guessing the number of Smarties in a jar, and bought a bundle of old comics from the book stall. Eric concentrated on keeping close to Roy, while watching out for his mum and Emily. They were likely to be around somewhere, although the fancy-dress wasn't due until four o'clock. From time to time Mr Blocker's voice boomed out over the public address. He welcomed everybody to the sports, and reminded them there was a refreshment area near the pavilion. He urged them to buy raffle tickets and mentioned Councillor Beanland. He told 'certain boys' to cease their interference with the groundsman's sprinkler.

At twenty past two Eric and Roy went up onto the grass bank. Eric was grateful to be out of the crowd and welcomed the chance to rest his little legs. Furthermore, at the back of the bank there was an area of much longer grass which would make a useful hiding place, if the need arose. Eric lay with his head on his paws and shut his eyes against the glare of the sun. He thought about the scene in the park. Sooner or later Joan and Alison were going to guess, if Roy didn't actually *tell* them, that is. He would have to talk to Roy. He thought about his mum and dad, and the trouble he'd be in when he got home.

Roy, meanwhile, was propped up on his elbows having a quick look at his comics. He was also eating a sherbet dip, and – apparently – thinking about Eric. 'Don't get distemper, Eric,' he said. 'They give you a needle in y'bum!'

At that moment a voice said, 'Excuse me!' Eric and Roy looked up. A large woman in a red dress was standing beside them. She was out of breath from climbing the bank. She said, 'Excuse me, but is this your dog?'

'Er ... yes,' said Roy.

'Don't mind me asking, but ... what d'you call him?'

'Er ... Rex,' said Roy. He couldn't bring himself to say 'Eric'.

'Oh!' The woman looked disappointed; embarrassed, too. 'Is he a smart dog, is he?'

'Very,' said Roy. 'He understands every word I say.'

'I can believe it,' said the woman.

Then another, smaller, woman in a green dress at the bottom of the bank joined in. 'Come on, Frances – I want a cup of tea!'

'Coming!' said the first woman. And then, 'Don't mind me asking, but has he ever ... done any sort of funny business with his paw?' She lowered her voice, '... Sort of *writing* like?'

Then Eric guessed who she was, and so did Roy.

'No,' he said.

'Oh!' said the woman.

'Frances!' said the other woman.

'Coming!' said Frances. She turned and began to descend the bank. '"Rex", you said.'

Roy nodded.

She reached the bottom, linked arms with her friend and went away.

As soon as she'd gone, Roy said, 'That was the woman who saw you writing, wasn't it?'

'Woof!' said Eric.

'I think I put her off, though.'

'Woof!' Eric said.

Then Roy said, 'Hey – it's starting!'

Eric scrambled to his feet. Down on the track, Mr Blocker in his best suit was escorting Councillor Beanland to the starting line. 'Come on Frobisher!' shouted Roy. (The woman in the red dress had vanished from his thoughts.) 'Frobisher' was one of the house teams, the others being Raleigh, Nelson and Drake. Councillor Beanland raised her pistol, the race began, the crowd cheered – Frobisher came nowhere.

After that Roy returned to his comics, while keeping a close watch on his friend, just in case. It crossed his mind that Eric could do with a collar and lead, though he doubted if he'd agree. Eric, for a time, remained on his feet and continued to look around. On the track he could see Mrs Jessop herding half a dozen infant girls in sacks behind the starting line. Another teacher, Mrs Tucker, was putting the scores up on a blackboard near the judges' table. Mr Moody, in *his* best suit, was preparing to start the second race. Farther off, a boy

– it might have been Hopper – was climbing onto the pavilion roof. In the distance, traffic was passing in the Bowles Road. The woman in the red dress was nowhere to be seen. Eric moved closer to Roy and began reading over his shoulder.

Eric and Roy stayed on the bank for another ten minutes. During this time Roy bundled up his comics and put them in his bag, read the label on his bottle of ketchup, finished the sherbet dip and watched a couple of races. (He was in no hurry to get changed for his own; the relays were the last events.) Eric watched the races, too. He also gave more thought to his situation without thinking of anything new. At one point he resisted the urge to scratch himself with a back leg.

Then at three o'clock something happened. A rather gruff voice came out over the public address. 'We have a message here about a missing child.' The voice belonged to Mr Hodge. 'It's a little girl – three years old – dressed in a ... what?' Someone, it appeared, was giving him the details. 'A Bo-Peep costume.'

Immediately Eric leapt to his feet.

'Her name is Emily and she was last seen a few minutes ago in the ... where? The toddlers' playground.'

Roy leapt to his feet, too. 'Did y'hear that?'

'Woof!' said Eric. He was already scrambling down the bank.

'Anyone seeing this child, please bring her to the announcer's table. Thank you.'

The toddlers' playground was a patch of grass with the pavilion on one side and the refreshment area on the other. It contained a climbing frame, a wooden slide, two little bikes, three pedal cars, a Wendy house, and some large building blocks – all borrowed for the day from the Tividale Nursery. A teacher from the nursery was there to keep an eye on things, helped by a couple of older girls from the comprehensive.

When Eric – closely followed by Roy – arrived, he

131

found a considerable crush of people. Most of them were on their way to get a cup of tea, or on their way from having had one. In the playground a number of small children were ... playing; one of them was Malky Biggs. Eric trotted forward and, almost without thinking, began to sniff around. He could smell grass, and warm wood, and tea. He could smell the nursery teacher's perfume, although she'd left to join the search for Emily.

Roy crouched beside him. 'How're we doing, Eric? Found anything?'

Eric made no reply, but continued to follow his nose. He could smell doughnuts and cigarette smoke. Eric had read about dogs and their sense of smell: how they could pick up the trail of a fox or a convict, or a truffle, even. At the time he hadn't really understood how it was done. Now he was beginning to find out. He could smell suntan oil and privet.

Then, as he approached the wooden slide, one of the comprehensive girls spotted him. She frowned and said – to Roy – 'No dogs!'

'Right!' said Roy. 'I'll get him.'

Eric heard all this and ignored it. He could smell cloth, and warm wood again, and ... he gave a sudden bark of triumph, *Emily*!

Emily's smell was a mixture of her mother's talc (that Emily loved to use), her grandma's kitchen floor polish, Emily's plastic sandals, Emily's feet and ..: Emily! (Everyone, he now remembered reading, had his own personal smell – like fingerprints.)

'Nearly got him!' said Roy, in answer to more frowns from the comprehensive girls. But Eric was picking up speed and looking anything but got. Nose

first – like a small brown Hoover – he skimmed across the grass. The pattern of Emily's trail led this way and that. She had played on everything, it seemed.

When Eric had read about dogs following trails, the thing that had puzzled him (and Roy) most was: how did the dog know which end of the trail was which? However, now that he was required to do it himself, it proved to be no problem at all. Emily's trail was like a dotted line drawn on the ground. It faded in the direction she'd come from, and was stronger in the direction she'd gone. Nor did Eric have trouble with the other trails – Malky's, for instance – which criss-crossed Emily's. The more he followed hers, the more tuned in he was to it (like a radio signal), and the less interference he got from other 'stations'.

Emily's trail, as it turned out, was short. It led out of the toddlers' playground, past the pavilion, twice round the unattended Punch and Judy tent, back towards the pavilion, up onto the pavilion steps, down again, up again, down again, and – finally – *behind* the pavilion. During this time Roy kept as close to Eric as he could. He tried to give the appearance of being in charge. Now and then he got funny looks from passers-by.

The path at the side of the pavilion was narrow and hemmed in by two cricket-pitch rollers and an enormous mower. There was a machine for marking white lines, the powerful smell of which temporarily

threw Eric off the scent and made him sneeze. Fortunately, by this time he hardly needed a scent. He blinked – his eyes were watering – continued down the path and turned a corner.

Eric now found himself in a small triangular space fenced in on two sides with the back of the pavilion making the third. This space contained a pile of wooden stakes and some coils of rope. It also contained Emily and a huge bull-mastiff.

The mastiff was looking fiercely (or so it seemed to Eric) at Emily. Emily was looking benignly at the mastiff. Worse still, she was approaching it with both hands out as though she meant to cuddle it. Eric didn't hesitate. He gave a brave bark – and leapt to the rescue.

18

See Him Off!

Eric had no real plan in mind except to put himself between Emily and the mastiff. (It was the same one he'd had trouble with before, from Stone Street.) However, the moment he did this, events moved rapidly and carried him along. The mastiff, though caught off guard, took a step forward and snarled. Eric stood his ground. (Roy clutched his bag and looked for something to throw.) Eric felt the fur rising along his back (for a second he thought he was changing again). A growl developed in his throat.

Emily said, 'Two dogs!'

Roy said, 'See him off, Eric!'

Eric said, 'Woof!'

Whereupon – unbelievably – the mastiff gave a sudden terror-stricken howl, turned tail, cleared the back fence with a tremendous jump, and disappeared.

In the silence which followed, Eric could hear the distant clatter of teacups, the sharp bang of the starter's pistol, the crowd cheering. He felt greatly puzzled, but elated, too. He had to check himself from advancing on the fence and barking through it.

Roy's first thought was that Eric must have said something to the mastiff. (He still believed that Eric could communicate with other dogs.) He was also, of course, bowled over with admiration. However, his final theory (developed later) was that the mastiff may have sensed – by smell, for instance, or a 'foreign accent' in Eric's barking – that here was no ordinary dog. Here was a zombie dog, perhaps, or a vampire dog – a body-snatcher dog! That'd be enough to scare a Dobermann Pinscher even!

Emily, meanwhile, was unperturbed. Having seen one dog depart, she simply transferred her interest, not to say affection, to the next. This one was more her size, anyway.

Roy said, 'Did y'see that bit of chain hanging from his collar? He's broken loose, I bet!'

'Woof!' said Eric.

Over her shoulder, and with all her attention fixed on Eric, Emily said, 'Hello, Roy!' She crouched and patted Eric on the head. He, for his part, felt a sudden urge to lick his little sister's face, and did so. She tasted of make-up (her red Bo-Peep cheeks) and banana yoghurt. Emily was charmed. She kissed him back (on the nose) and peered closely into his face. 'Nice dog,' she said. And then, 'Eric?'

'Eric's not here!' said Roy, intervening sharply. He had the uncomfortable feeling Emily was onto

something. 'Come on, let's have an ice-cream, and find y'mum.'

Roy certainly had a way with small children; he understood them, too, as the casual mention of ice-cream showed. Emily was hooked: 'Or a lolly!' she said.

So Roy took Emily's hand and led her, via the refreshment area (where lollies and ice-cream were also sold), to the announcer's table. Eric followed at a distance; he wasn't keen to meet his mum. Emily, though intent on her lolly, kept swivelling round to see if he was there.

Then Mr Hodge made an announcement saying Emily was safe and sound. Shortly after, a hot and flustered Mrs Banks came rushing up. She was out of breath and encumbered by a home-made shepherd's crook. 'Oh, Emily, where've you been? Did you find her, Roy? You are good! Where's Eric?' Mrs Banks gave Emily a cuddle and a telling-off.

'He's, er . . . still looking – we split up,' said Roy.

'I only left her for a minute,' said Mrs Banks, turning to Mr Hodge.

'Two dogs!' said Emily.

'Little Bo-Peep lost herself,' said Mr Hodge.

'A big dog and a little dog!' Emily said.

Then, even more hot and flustered, and encumbered by a home-made sheep on wheels, Emily's gran came rushing up. 'Oh, Emily!'

Mr Hodge offered his chair and gratefully Emily's gran sat down. She fanned herself with a programme. 'Look at her,' she said, nodding at Emily. 'She's not bothered.'

Emily remained engrossed in her lolly. 'A big dog and a little dog,' she said.

'Yes, dear,' said her gran.

And Emily said, 'I want one.'

Now Emily's gran spotted Roy. He was trying to sneak off. 'Hello, Roy – where's Eric?'

'I only left her for a minute,' said Mrs Banks. And then, 'Yes – where *is* Eric? Can't face me, I'll bet!'

'I'll find him for you,' said Roy, continuing to back away.

'Tell him I'd like a word,' said Mrs Banks.

'Right!' said Roy.

'And Roy?'

'Yes?'

'One more thing: what's Eric wearing?'

'Wearing?'

'Yes. As far as I can tell, he's running round with nothing on.'

Then Roy experienced the guilty feeling he sometimes had with his own mum, made worse on this occasion by the fact that he himself was innocent. 'Wearing ... I can't remember.' At which point, out of range of further questioning, he turned and fled.

Eric had watched all this (and heard most of it) from his hiding place a short way off, under the tombola table. His mother's comment reminded him, if he needed reminding, of the trouble he was in and the risks he ran. He had another, more urgent, problem, too: thirst. He was panting so hard he sounded like a piece of wood being sawn up.

As Roy went by, Eric slipped out and followed him. After they'd gone a few yards, Roy stopped and bent down. 'Y'did great, Eric!' he said. 'Hey, you're looking thirsty.'

'Get me a drink, then,' thought Eric.

'You want a drink?'

'Woof!'

'Right,' said Roy. 'Let's see what we can do.' He turned once more in the direction of the refreshment area. 'Perhaps we can find you a saucer or something.'

Meanwhile, out on the track, Mr Moody – using twice the words he was accustomed to use – was starting a race. 'Ready, steady ...' He held the pistol aloft – bang!

Elsewhere, Hopper – watched by most of the large Hopper family – was behaving himself in the high jump. Mr Hodge was making an announcement about the Boys' Brigade band. Overhead a few clouds had gathered and a plane was flying by.

Eric and Roy had almost reached the refreshment area, when suddenly Eric felt a *wobbly* sensation in his legs. He remembered the last time this had happened, in Roy's room, just before ... 'Oh, no!' He remembered reading about dogs and earthquakes. They often ran away minutes before it happened. They knew it was coming. *He* knew it was coming. 'I'm changing back!'

Desperately – there were people everywhere – Eric looked for a place to hide. He felt like Cinderella at twelve o'clock. He'd never make it to the long grass, that was for sure. Then, up ahead, he caught sight of the Punch and Judy tent. It was still unattended, though a scattering of hopeful infants sat waiting for the show. 'That'll do,' he thought, and thereafter instantly shot past Roy like a whippet, burrowed frantically at the back of the tent, wriggled under – and disappeared.

Roy's first reaction, having witnessed this, was to hope no one else had. When he was sure they hadn't, he casually approached the tent, bent down and pretended to search in his bag. 'Eric, come out of there!' Roy spoke from the side of his mouth, in his usual classroom manner. There was no reply. He said, 'Anyway, what's it like?' (forgetting that Eric couldn't tell him), 'I've always wondered.'

What it was like, of course, was the inside of a tall, brightly coloured tent. The little curtain at the top, where the puppets appeared, was drawn. The light was green and turquoise and red, where the sun shone through the canvas material. The puppets themselves dangled upside down from a row of hooks on a piece of wood waist-high at the front of the tent. There was a small wooden box for the puppeteer to stand on. Eric, however, was in no condition to notice any of this, or tell Roy about it. He was

otherwise engaged in changing back into a boy. Also his eyes were shut.

Roy, meanwhile, was becoming impatient. 'Come on, Eric, I thought you were thirsty!' And suspicious, too. 'What're you doing in there?'

Still there was no answer. Roy shuffled sideways and put his ear to the tent: nothing. Then, just as he was wondering what else to do, a *hand* appeared under the bottom edge, and a voice – Eric's – said, 'Lend me y'kit, Roy.'

19

The Jigsaw Theory

Eric became a boy again in the Punch and Judy tent at 3.35 p.m. The timetable after that was as follows:

3.40   Eric emerged and was caught in the act by Mrs Jessop, who had 'something to say'.

3.45   Eric got his drink, but was too late to take part in the long jump.

3.53   Hopper won the high jump but broke the cane.

4.00   Joan and Alison created a problem in the girls' three-legged race. Having qualified for the final with different partners, they now expected to run together.

4.10   The clouds grew darker and a light drizzle began to fall. Emily came joint fourth in a speeded-up fancy-dress parade and won a set of felt pens.

4.12   Roy ran in the relay. Mr Blocker had 'something to say' about his lack of kit. He refused Roy permission to run in his hat.

4.20   A roll of thunder was heard.

4.24   Raleigh was declared the overall winning house, and a provisional P.T.A. profit of £263.00 was announced.

4.30   The rain fell more heavily. Eric and Roy set off for home.

On the way they took shelter once or twice in shop doorways when the rain fell even more heavily. Among other things they discussed Roy's 'zombie dog' theory, whether Emily had really recognized Eric when he was a dog, the contents of a chemist's window ('Bags that diabetic chocolate!') and, finally, in Clay Street, Eric's alibi.

Eric said, 'Y'see, what they'll think is, I left the back door open and the TV on, went out without my clothes or kit, and let a dog get in! How can I explain that?'

'Say you forgot,' said Roy. He flicked the rain from his hat. 'Or did it for a bet or something.'

'Did what for a bet?'

'Anything – all of it. That's what I'd say.'

Of course, from one point of view, Eric's best alibi would have been the truth. At least that way there'd be no need to make anything up, or risk of forgetting what he'd already said. Unfortunately, it was a bit late for the truth, in Eric's opinion. Besides, his mum and dad would never believe him. They'd think he was making the *truth* up.

So Eric arrived home and, in due course, told his story. He'd done it for a dare, he said. Roy had come round ... he'd put Roy's kit on ... Roy had run off with his apple ... Eric had chased him up the road. Then later, Roy had lost his watch ... and they'd looked for it ... and by that time ... Eric rambled on,

144

surprising even himself with his own inventiveness. His mum, however, was less impressed. 'That's the biggest rigmarole I ever heard,' she said. 'What happened really?'

Eric's punishments – when they finally came – were a telling-off from his mum, and a long speech from his dad about dogs getting in who could easily have been burglars ('A gorilla could get in!' Emily said), and TV sets blowing up, and the danger of wearing other people's clothes. He was sent to bed early on Saturday, kept in on Sunday and scrutinized more closely than ever by his mum for much of the following week.

When Eric and Roy met on the paper-round on Monday, Roy said, 'What did they say?'

Eric told him.

Then Roy revealed that *he'd* had a telling-off for lending his kit. Then he said, 'Listen, I saw Kenny yesterday; his cousin had a video. Guess what it was?'

'What?'

'"Dr Jekyll and Mr Hyde"!'

'Never heard of it.'

'Nor me,' said Roy. 'But Kenny says it's about this man – this scientist – who drinks this stuff and turns into this other man.'

'What stuff?'

'I don't know, a potion or something. So, anyway, I've been thinking – perhaps that's it.'

But Eric was unconvinced. He hadn't drunk many potions lately, he said.

Later, on the way to school, Eric told Roy about an idea he'd had, or rather was beginning to have. It had occurred to him first on Sunday morning while he was eating his breakfast, part of which was a boiled egg. 'I was thinking: eggs turn into chickens, don't they? And nobody says that's strange. And chrysalises turn into butterflies –'

'And tadpoles into frogs,' said Roy.

'Yes ... and all that – and yet a boy turns into a dog and that's strange.'

'Well, it *is* strange,' said Roy.

They crossed the road and entered the front playground. A game of mass football was in progress; fourth years against the rest.

Eric said, 'I don't know, I mean, you could say everything's strange.'

'Or nothing is,' said Roy.

'Yes. I mean, I bet a Martian'd think a boiled egg was strange.'

'He might not,' said Roy. 'He might look like one.'

A rush of players went by and Eric missed this last remark (or chose to ignore it). 'Or a safety-pin!' he said. 'Or a blade of grass!'

'He'd think you changing into a dog was stranger,' Roy said.

During assembly Roy asked Eric if a Martian would think Mr Blocker was strange. Later, in the classroom, he rolled his trouser leg up to show Eric how strange knees were, and got a fierce look from Mrs Jessop. After that there were distractions. Mrs Jessop was in an energetic mood. There was a fire drill at ten o'clock, and more mass football at playtime, into which Eric and Roy (not to mention Mr Hodge and Mr Moody) got drawn. There was a meeting for school-camp children at lunch-time, and in the afternoon a talk for the third years from a man who wrote children's books.

Eric, however, found time to think about things even if he didn't manage to discuss them with Roy. It still seemed to him that strangeness was a strange business. On the way home, as he passed Russell's sweet shop (without looking in), he said, 'I've been thinking.'

'Me, too,' said Roy.

'What if strange things happened all the time.'

'That'd be very strange,' said Roy.

'No, it wouldn't, that's the point, it'd be *normal*. It'd be like if everybody had two heads; nobody'd think twice about it.'

'They'd all think twice if they had two heads,' said

147

Roy. He was balancing along the wall outside the Old People's Home. Eric jumped up and followed him. They watched a police car going down Joining's Bank.

Roy said, 'I've got a better idea. Perhaps every time you turn into a dog, somewhere in the universe some poor dog is turning into you!'

Eric considered this for a moment. It wasn't bad.

Roy said, 'Like a sort of jigsaw, maybe, with a picture on both sides – and your bit just gets turned over now and then.'

'And it's got a dog on the back,' said Eric.

'Yes!'

Roy dropped off the wall. Eric followed. They stepped aside to let a woman with a wide pushchair (with twins and shopping in it) go by. Eric kicked a cigarette packet into the gutter. 'Who's doing the turning, though?' he said.

20

Little Lucy

For the next few days, Eric and Roy continued to swop ideas. They made notes and, in Roy's case, tracings to put in the Dog File. They argued about wasting Eric's file paper. (Roy had a habit of starting again, if he made the least mistake.) They argued about which was the best theory. Eric had added 'THE POTION THEORY' (at Roy's insistence) and 'THE JIGSAW THEORY' to the list.

Then on Friday something happened. Eric and his family were having their tea in the kitchen when there was a knock at the door and his gran came in. 'Oh, having your tea, are you?' She had an excited, but also rather sheepish look on her face. She was carrying a cardboard box which she placed on the floor.

'Hello, Gran!' said Eric.

And his dad said, 'What've you got there?'

Emily, meanwhile, had immediately left the table and gone over to the box.

Eric's gran made no reply, but put a finger to her lips. To Emily she said, 'You have a look!' Whereupon Emily pulled back the folded top of the box (it was a Walker's crisp box) and peeped inside. As she did so, a small, rather anxious-looking brown-and-white puppy peeped out. 'A dog!' Emily turned and

149

beamed a dazzling smile at her mum and dad. 'A little dog!'

'Before you say anything,' said Eric's gran, 'you don't have to keep it. It can stop with me, if you like. Emily can come round. It'll be hers, but I'll look after it.'

But, of course, once the puppy had licked a few hands, had a little bark, and generally shown *his* pleasure in *their* company, they did keep him. Mr Banks complained about grandparents spoiling children, and promised to get his own back on Emily when she had hers. Mrs Banks said she might have preferred an older, slower dog. But for all that, by the end of the evening the puppy was well on the way to becoming an established member of the family.

In the days that followed, Mr Banks bought him a

collar and lead, and Mrs Banks bought him a basket. Roy – as soon as he heard the news – bought him a rubber bone. (Actually, he'd got it already, with another dog in mind.) Eric took him, and Emily, for frequent walks in the park. And Emily christened him. As a matter of fact, she christened him twice: 'Lucy Banks' to begin with, and 'Monty' following some persuasion from the others.

On the Wednesday after school, Eric and Roy were sitting on Eric's back step watching Emily in her sandpit. Monty was temporarily asleep in the kitchen; his little belly bulging like a grape from recent eating.

'Look at her,' said Roy. 'You'd think she was being paid!'

Emily was digging vigorously, and bustling about with buckets and jelly moulds. At that moment Monty came clambering over them. He galloped across the grass and flopped into the sandpit. Emily at once abandoned her digging, wiped her sandy hands on the lawn and gave him a hug.

'She's really mad about dogs, your sister is,' said Roy. He smiled. 'Hey, I just thought – it could be *her*, y'know.'

'What could?' Eric was flicking at nearby flower heads with the puppy's lead.

'Emily!' said Roy, and he laughed. 'It could be her thought waves that's causing it. She'd rather have a dog than a brother!'

Eric laughed, too. He gave Roy a shove and stood up. 'Come on, Emily – time for a walk!'

And Roy said, 'That's it all right: *The Power of Wishing*!'

Half an hour later Eric and Roy sat on a bench in the park. Emily, with Monty on a lead, was running round them in ever widening circles. A short way off a game of cricket was in progress. The players included Philip Dobson and his friends again, and Kenny Biggs, and Hopper. As usual, there was as much quarrelling as cricket. All the players were umpires, of course, but Hopper was the chief of the umpires. His decisions were, at times, eccentric. Now and then he appeared to tackle an opposing batsman from his position at short square leg.

But on this occasion, Eric and Roy were less interested in cricket and more interested in Emily. She was some distance away by now, standing still and looking back at them. She seemed quite tiny and insignificant (Monty was pretty well invisible) against the broad spread of the park pitches with the tall poplars behind.

Roy, however, was not deceived. 'Look at her,' he said, and shaded his eyes with his hand. 'The brains behind the whole thing!'

21

Then This Happened

Whether Emily was the brains behind the whole thing or not, isn't known. What *is* known is that from the time she got her dog, Eric never changed again, or at least he hasn't so far.

In Roy's opinion this was a very telling point. ('She gets her dog – you stop changing – it proves it!') But he was uncertain and confused, too. After all, in the beginning he'd only said it was Emily for a joke. Also, he actually preferred other, more macabre theories; and besides, his *hopes* were that Eric *would* change again.

Eric, for his part, didn't dismiss THE EMILY THEORY; he rather liked it, in fact. However, it was the idea that strange things simply happened once in a while, which most convinced him at the time, and still does. In his opinion – especially as he grew older – in this world a bit of abnormality was probably normal.

But, of course, for the first couple of weeks Eric still expected to change. He even hid spare clothes in the garage just in case. (Mrs Banks discovered them two days later and wondered what was up.) Roy, too, had high hopes, especially of the school camp. ('That's the place, Eric – the woods!') But the camp came and went without incident; and Eric's cousin

Marion returned to her paper-round, and the school term ended, and the holidays began.

After that Eric and Roy became fourth years in Mr Hodge's class. On the first day of term some of his previous class came back for a visit. They looked half-proud, half-embarrassed in their new school clothes: dresses and blazers, ties and scarves. Hopper – tattooless, but with his tie in his pocket – was among them.

As the months went by, Roy continued, from habit, to keep an eye on his friend. Then, in the new year, a new girl arrived in the class and Roy kept an eye on her instead. During this period both boys could feel their memories of the 'dog days' fading. They made strenuous efforts to hang on to them, as people often do with a good dream. But time kept passing, and fresh dramas arrived (a burglary at the scout hut; a ghost at the school camp) to push the old ones out.

Now it's nearly three years later. Eric hasn't changed into a dog again, but other changes have occurred. His cousin Marion is engaged. Emily is six and soon to be a Brownie. Eric has grown five inches and become less in awe of his mum's detective work. Roy (slightly the older of the two) has turned into a teenager. He combs his hair a dozen times a day, and has lately taken Joan Spooner to the pictures.

But even now, occasionally, something happens which ... take last week, for instance. Eric had gone on a visit with his combined studies group (Roy was in a different group) to the Bell Street R.S.P.C.A. dogs' home. Here he'd seen the vets at work, and the kennelmaids ... and various dogs. One in particular caught his attention. It was sitting a little apart

Here boy

from the others in its pen, was noticeably calm and
had some of the features of a Norfolk terrier.

Eric crouched in front of it and ran his fingers over
the wire mesh. 'Here, boy!' he said. Then – almost
without thinking (but with a quick look over his
shoulder) – he added, '*Are* you a boy? Bark once for
"yes"; twice for "no".'

The dog put its head on one side and pricked an
ear. It allowed the top of its head to be scratched.
'Woof!' it said.